Table of C

Alkali's Monster

Zachary Kuhl

Published by Kuhl Books, 2024.

ALKALI'S MONSTER

First edition. September 22, 2024.

Copyright © 2024 Zachary Kuhl.

ISBN: 979-8227283283

Written by Zachary Kuhl.

For every young soul that gave me the chance to try and be someone else for a week or two every summer growing up. Your patience in my lack of maturity and grace in seasonal friendship has never been forgotten.

It's War This Year

There's a certain air of fuck-it-all and be-who-you-want that comes with summer camp. If you're lucky and play your cards right, you could find yourself in a situation to reinvent yourself once a year every year with a whole new audience and maybe a handful of good friends. Not everyone has the luxury of experiencing that, but those of us who did understand how precious it is. We also understand how fragile it can be.

The opposite experience is getting sent away from your home to some far-off place and being denied the opportunity to try on new personalities. Instead of being lucky and having a handful of friends to go through the motions with, you draw the short straw and get stuck with the perennial bully who will be there every third week in June to remind everyone of the time you blew chunks all over Sarah Coughlin when you were twelve.

I was that unlucky.

In the summer between seventh and eighth grade, I begged and pleaded for my mom to not send me packing, but she wasn't having it. My mother was a lot of things, but understanding wasn't on that list. She valued her quiet time, so when I wasn't in school, I was playing basketball, failing miserably at baseball, making a fool of myself in the school play, pretending I understood the rules of chess club, or was at summer camp. By modern standards, she may have been considered a tiger mom, except she didn't give a shit if I was good or not, as long as I was out of the house.

With that being her primary driver for deciding what should be done with me at any given season, I was sent to four different summer camps each year, one after the other, with perhaps a weekend break in between. These camps weren't close to home either; she preferred the ones where she could take a detour to an outlet mall after dropping me off.

First was basketball camp in Hays, KS, then there was a Christian Bible camp outside Grand Island, NE. After that, I made a two-week stop at a camp for wannabe child actors outside Kansas City, MO, and finally a week and a half stay at the wilderness camp my father insisted I attended, Camp Alkali. It was tucked neatly along the edge of the Nebraska National Forest and felt the farthest from my hometown of Kearney, Nebraska. Camp Alkali was a proper wilderness camp, complete with a supposed monster living in the lake, rumors of an old outlaw hideout in the woods, and a do-or-die culture to make the whole experience that much more traumatic for us all.

"Mom, please, I don't want to go!" I pleaded from the back seat of my mom's van, which was struggling to navigate the gravel road that led to the entrance of the camp.

"You know how important it is for you to get out, be a boy, poke a frog, and explore the woods. Things like that. Besides, I didn't drive all this way with your nagging to give up now." She took a drag off her cigarette, then flicked the butt out of her window.

"But what if he's there again this year? He almost killed me last year, and we got in huge trouble! Remember? I rolled my ankle!"

"First off, rolling your ankle isn't a near-death injury; it just means you're clumsy. Second, you didn't get banned, so it couldn't have been that bad. You're getting yourself worked up over nothing." She wasn't open to any argument I could make; that much was clear.

Before I could think of a last-ditch effort to evade my fate, Mom turned the van onto a side road that rolled under an oversized wooden arch that said "Camp Alkali" on a large cedar plank. Animal skulls decorated the space on the rest of the arch, and through its entry point, you could see the bulk of the camp. It should have been a beautiful or exciting sight to a boy like me, but all I could think about was the year before and how poorly it went.

That particular camp was a mixed bag for me when I was growing up. On one hand, I had found a small group of friends who I could look forward to: Diego Connors, Barry Griffiths, and Rodney Hughes. We'd all met there our first year, the summer after fourth grade, and managed to keep in touch mostly through letters and an occasional phone call. Looking at us from the outside, our little group didn't make much sense, but we found enough common ground to build on.

On the other hand, I had to be wary of, and mentally prepare for, Dexter Hansley and his gang of knuckle draggers. Dexter found a new group each summer, seemingly drawing the rowdiest kids at camp like moths to a flame. Occasionally, there'd be a holdover from the year prior, but it was mostly fresh meat each summer. He and I had been at odds for years, and I didn't expect that year to be any different.

Mom kept the van on track, passing under the looming arch and down the road to the camp's main hub. The campus itself was modest, consisting of a mess hall, a gymnasium, a small office that doubled as a nurses station, and six cabins—three boys and three girls, each housing ten campers. Camp Alkali took pride in its deteriorating exterior, so every off-season someone would come through and paint all the buildings a new color, that year was Forrest Green, which made the siding of each building look like it was bowing, pulling itself to the ground.

The van rolled in front of the mess hall where registration was set up inside, and Mom hopped out of the van, prepared to drag me out by force if necessary. It wasn't. She pulled the door open, and I stepped out with my head slung in defeat. Mom fetched my suitcase from the truck and placed it on the curb before lighting another cigarette and crossing her arms to scold me.

"Listen, young man, we don't send you to all these camps for nothing, you know? You're supposed to learn something. Hell, even improve a bit, okay? So please try to buy into the program this year. Can you do that for me?" She took a long drag, then blew the smoke out of her nose like a skinny, subran, mini-van-driving dragon.

I grabbed my suitcase and turned away from her toward the mess hall. "No promises."

She didn't bother to argue, and I didn't blame her. We'd worked out an unspoken routine for these kinds of situations. Mom would ask me to not be me; I'd say fuck off, she'd get mad, I'd walk away, and she'd walk away; it was dysfunctional, but it kept the day moving. So without another word, a hug, a kiss, or a goodbye, she crawled into her driver's seat and drove off.

I made my way into the mess hall and waited in line behind a few other kids who were there. None of them looked familiar to me, but at that age, it was hard to say who was who. People aged and changed so much from year to year that their faces didn't stay static like they did in your memories. I waited there silently until I was called, entertaining myself by guessing the names of the kids in line ahead of me.

"Next!" An older lady sitting at a faded plastic table squawked. I took a stiff step toward her. "Name?" She asked in a raspy, definitely smoked as much as my mother, kind of voice.

"Matthews. Edward Matthews."

She used one of her oversized fake nails to scan her clipboard until she found my name, then crossed it out with a pen. "Alright, I got you right here. Says here that you were sent by your parents. That right?"

"Yes, ma'am, by my mother." I tried to keep my tone as upbeat as I could.

"Odd." She shot me a suspicious look. "They let you back in after last year?"

"Seems so, ma'am."

She raised a disapproving eyebrow at me. "So you know the drill, then?"

"I believe so."

"Good. You're in cabin C. Go get settled." Her finger pointed to a door I'd entered through, and I promptly carried my one bag with me out of it.

I hadn't even made it three feet out of the door when I heard the unmistakable east coast accent of Rodney Hughes. "Eddie! Eddie, is that you?"

He was jogging toward me across the parking lot, and I was shocked to see he was at least six feet tall. The summer before, we were the same height. "Rodney! Holy shit man, when'd you get this tall?"

Rodney was from Boston, but his parents sent him to Camp Alkali to make sure he learned some 'real-world skills'; otherwise, we would have never met. He was a first-generation American; his parents had moved to Boston from somewhere in Sudan; both were doctors. Out of our group of friends, Rodney was both the funny one and the tough one, which made him a type of social double threat, something he knew how to use to his advantage.

"I just take after my old man." He cracked a wide smile. "You just got here?"

"Yeah, my mom just dropped me off. Have you seen Deigo and Barry yet?" I tried to control my voice so as not to sound too eager.

"Yeah, yeah. They're in the cabin, I think."

"Cabin C?"

"You know it. After the shit that happened last year, you knew they were going to put us in The Hole." He let out a laugh loud enough to draw the attention of the other camps passing by, not that Rodney would have minded.

We walked together along the path that mirrored the lake banks, slowly making our way to our temporary home. There was a whole year's worth of life to catch up on, and each of us tried to hit the key points. I told him about my dog dying, my family changing churches, and my first kiss with Susan Katz (we didn't actually kiss, but I'd bragged about her being my girlfriend the year before, so I felt like I needed a follow-up story). He told me about his dad starting a new job, his new baby sister, and how weird things in Boston had felt since the twin towers fell during the school year. 9/11 shook the whole country; no one doubts that, but for many young people at the time, it felt like the world was titled on its axis a bit more after that day.

After about fifteen minutes, we were at the steps of Cabin C, nicknamed The Hole, because it was a true dumpster fire of a building. The roof leaked, the floorboard flexed, it housed a small city of ants, something lived in the walls (the debate of rat vs. mouse was never settled), and a family of raccoons had claimed the crawl space. Our home away from home was reserved for kids with 'behavioral issues' and the incident that my friends and Dexter's gang of nimrods caused got us all blacklisted, so as much as we hated it, The Hole was home.

"You know, all of the new campers will think we're a bunch of badasses once they hear the rumors about this cabin." Rodney remarked.

"Or they'll think we're idiots if they find out what actually happened." I said, making my way up the steps to the cabin door, which was barely hanging onto its hinges.

"History is written by the victors, Eddie; did you ever hear that?"

"You think we're the winners in this situation? We're staying in The Hole, Rodney."

I pulled the cabin's door open and stepped into its mildew-infested air. The first thing I saw was Diego Connors, his eyes wide with panic, motioning for me to duck. Unfortunately for me, I didn't listen, and instead I looked to my right and saw a fist coming at my face. The next thing I knew, I felt a stinging pain in my nose, heard a crunch, and then fell to my ass, hitting my head against the wall on my way down.

There wasn't even time for me to get my bearings before I heard Dexter's nasal voice mocking me. "It's war this year, Eddie! You hear me? Fucking war!"

Summer Of Servitude

"I gotta say, its seems like you really enjoy making an impression, Mr. Matthews, in the worst kind of way." Nurse Linda said while handing me an ice pack.

She was the camp nurse every year that I'd been there. An oversized woman with an oversized southern accent and an oversized beehive hairdo to complete her persona. Her nurses' station was set up in the corner of the office cabin and more closely resembled a civil war triage tent than a proper medical facility. The floors were covered in faded yellow carpets, the walls were bare wood planks, and a few cluttered desks dotted the space with rusting filing cabinets to match. There were four windows, two on each side wall, that let in light and the muffled noise of campers from outside, which gave the whole space a dull orange glow. As far as I could tell, the only new thing in the whole building was a poster of the Twin Towers pinned on a corkboard with the words 'Never Forget' printed in thick black letters.

I winched as I placed the ice pack on my face. "To be fair, I didn't start it this time."

Linda let out a deep, hearty laugh. "Sure, but I don't think the Director is gonna care much. You saw the beating your friends put on Mr. Hansley."

There was no denying that. I didn't see much after my head hit the wall, but from what I could make out, Rodney, Diego, and Barry jumped Dexter and didn't look like they were holding back. My vision had gone blurry, and I was distracted by the pain of my newly broken nose, so I wasn't particularly concerned with the details of the beatdown happening in front of me. I did notice, though, that Dexter didn't seem to have anyone to back him up, like he was lacking his usual entourage of minions.

"Dexter got a taste of his own medicine, so what?" I smirked a tad and was quickly punished for it with a searing pain across the bridge of my nose.

Nurse Linda didn't have the chance to scold me before the Camp Director waltzed in, with Dexter lagging behind him like a fat dog on a leash. The Director was a tall man with leathery skin, a bald head so devoid of hair it glittered under the sun, and a goatee that was so dark black that everyone agreed he must have dyed it in his off time. He'd served as Director at Camp Alkali since I started going there, but for all, I knew he had been there from day one; he certainly acted like he built the place, taking offense to any degradation of the camp's character or appearance.

"Eddie." His voice boomed as he crossed the room to his desk. "Pleasure as always. Making yourself known already, it seems?"

"Oh, you know me, Lester." I hopped off the small cot I was sitting on and followed him and Dexter to his desk. "I'm just making sure your job isn't too easy. We'd hate for you to get bored now, wouldn't we?"

He sat behind his desk and leveled an annoyed glare at me. "You may call me Director Downs."

Dexter and I had been in his office enough times to know the motions we'd have to go through in order to walk free, starting with sitting across from him in a pair of aging metal folding chairs. I gave Dexter a quick once-over and saw that Nurse Linda wasn't downplaying what had happened; my friends had given him a proper beating. He had a black eye, a few bruises on his face, a split lip, and a small collection of scrapes on his arms. I'd never seen Dexter in that kind of shape; it seemed to have brought him down a rung.

Director Downs took a deep breath and placed his hands on the table. "Here's the deal, boys. I've known the two of you since, well, since you started coming here, and I know you've never gotten along. But what happened today was too far."

Neither of us said anything; we just shot each other a dirty look, the pair of us silently praying for each other's heads to explode.

"After the incident you two caused last year, I don't feel comfortable having you around the other campers." He continued. "Which doesn't leave me with many options."

"I completely understand." The metal chair squeaked against the floor as I stood up. "I'll start packing."

"Sit down, Eddie." Director Downs demanded, hitting his fist on the desk, to drive his point home. "Neither of you are going home. I spoke with both your parents, and we all agree that it'd be best for you to stay here."

Dexter put his hands up and protested in his nasal voice, "The fuck is that supposed to mean? Just let me go home! I'm over this shit!"

"Dexter, use that language again, and I'll have you cleaning outhouses. Understand?"

Both Dexter and I sat in silence, slowly soaking in the gravity of our situation. Over the years, we'd been in Director Downs's office and been assigned to cleaning tasks and odd jobs as punishments for squabbles and pranks gone wrong, but over all those meetings, he'd never raised his voice like he did that day. We were in deep shit, no denying that.

"Understood," Dexter muttered under his breath.

"Good." Director Downs stood up, walked around the desk, and sat on its edge, looking down at us as he continued to speak. "You boys, including Rodney, Diego, and Barry, are being assigned to maintenance duties for the first five days of camp. If you boys do well and behave yourselves, you can go back to being regular campers for the last five days. Any questions?"

Dexter and I shared a concerned look before I spoke up. "What does that mean exactly? How are we supposed to know what to do?"

"You boys will be supervised by our new maintenance man, Mr. Green, and he's been given very specific instructions on what you are and are not allowed to be doing. So don't expect him to be an easy mark, you hear me?" Director Downs forced his eyes to open wider to make his point.

"We still stuck sleeping in The Hole?" Dexter dared to ask.

Director Down nodded his head aggressively. "Indeed. After your little outburst, Mr. Hansley, your assigned councilor resigned, so I've asked Mr. Green to move into Cabin C to serve as your full-time supervisor." He slapped his knee, pushed himself off the desk, and walked past us to the door. "Now, gentlemen, I have a camp to run, and you boys have work to do, so head back to your bunks and wait for instructions."

He opened the door that led outside and ushered us to leave. Dexter got up first, and I followed behind, wondering if I sucker punched him, could I end up in more trouble, or would I still be in the same situation? I didn't let the thought linger, mostly because Nurse Linda was waving goodbye and mouthing the words 'behave yourself' as I walked to the door, which led to five days of hard labor.

Director Downs did not say another word; he only slammed the door behind us, and Dexter and I were alone on the path. Neither of us spoke for a while as we began the small journey from the office back to The Hole; instead, we took in the sights of things our lives would be void of for the next few days: kids canoeing on the lake, a group of girls reading and whispering to each other under a tree, a couple of boys practicing with bows, things like that. I couldn't speak for Dexter, but I was willing to bet he felt like I did—bitter.

"This is all your fault, Eddie." He eventually said this as our cabin began to come into sight.

"You hit me, jackass! I didn't even want to be here this year."

"Me either!" He agreed. "After all the shit you caused last year, I knew coming back was a bad idea."

"I caused?" My voice cracked a bit from the frustration. "None of it would have happened if you just fucked off like I told you to."

My gut told me to punch him, even though I knew it'd only lead to more trouble. I just craved some form of justice for the years of torment he'd put me through. Before I could though, Dexter stopped dead in his tracks and peered out at the lake. His face was twisted up in confusion, and I could see him gnawing on his cheek in contemplation.

"What are you looking at?" I asked.

Dexter didn't break his stare at the lake. "I just, uh, just thought I saw something over there. Something big, I think."

He was baiting me, no doubt about it; everyone who'd been to Camp Alkali more than once knew the campfire stories about the lake monster. In my first year, a few of the counselors got together to build a fake monster out of some spare canoes and scrap wood and got a whole herd of fourth graders to dash for shore, screaming for their lives. What was his plan? Get me to ask what he saw and make fun of me for being gullible. Or maybe I'd walk over to the shore with him and he'd shove me in? Whatever it was, I wasn't falling for it; there was no Alkali Lake Monster.

"Ha. Ha. Ha. Very funny, Dexter." I kept walking toward the cabin.

"I'm serious." He protested before shaking his head and catching up with me. "It doesn't matter. But, hey, I got to know, how'd you know Downs's name was Lester?"

"I saw his driver's license once. It was my second year here, and he'd dropped his wallet during a staff versus campers tug of war game." I'd almost forgotten about that memory, but in that moment, it felt like I was reliving it. "The only reason I found it was because you shoved me in the mud. We'd lost to the staff, and you came right over to me with that tall blonde kid who had those bright green glasses. What was his name?"

"Brandon Stuckley," Dexter answered. "I remember him. He was a mean son of a bitch, but I don't think I ever saw him after that year."

"Right, Brandon. He was mean—really fucking mean. The two of you told me I was the reason we lost, you called me shrimpy and shoved me into the mud." I paused for a moment and almost felt like crying. The feelings of that day felt like they were right under the surface. "Anyways, when I fell in the mud, I felt something hard under me, and it was the wallet. I looked inside and saw it said Lester Downs, so I found him and gave it to him. Ever since then, every once in a while, he would be cool with me calling him Lester."

"But not today, huh?"

"Obviously."

We'd finally arrived at the foot of the cabin steps and made our way inside. Rodney and Barry were lying in their bunks when we entered, both of them looking bored out of their minds. Barry was the only one who seemed to realized that we entered, and he jumped up and almost knocked me over with a bear hug.

"Eddie! You're alive!" He said, squeezing me so tight that I thought my eyes were going to pop from my skull.

Barry and I took some time to warm up to each other, but once we did, we would have gone to war for each other. He was from Colorado, some small town he rarely mentioned because no one knew where it was, and he may have been the most prepared kid for a wilderness camp. Everyone who met Barry learned quickly that he knew what he was doing and that it was wise to take his advice. Even Dexter was known to listen to him from time to time.

"Yeah, what of it?" I responded, struggling for breath.

"I thought you were a goner for sure." Barry put me down, and I took a deep breath of the cabin's stale air. "That's why we had to beat little Dexy here back to the stone age." Barry flashed him a grin.

"Fuck you, Griffith." Dexter said as he crawled into his bunk, flipping us the bird for good measure.

"So you heard the news?" He asked with wide eyes. "We're stuck on maintenance duty."

"Yeah, I heard. And we're getting babysat by some janitor?" Barry shrugged. "That's what we heard."

Rodney spoke up from his bunk. "You think he'll be some cranky old geezer?"

"Probably. Sure as hell won't be some hot chick; we ain't that lucky." I responded, grinning at my own joke. Then something dawned on me. "Where's Diego?"

"He snuck off to meet up with Megan Drakos." Barry said with a wide grin, clearly excited to gossip about Deigo's questionable taste in girls. "You remember her? The crazy chick from last year? Apparently, they've been pen pals."

Rodney sat up in his bunk and shook his head. "That bitch is crazy; he's going to get himself in deep shit hanging around her."

Before Barry or I could agree, we heard a distant but clear message coming from the camp intercom system outside the cabin. "Attention. Attention. All members of Cabin C, please report to the mess hall. Repeat. All members of Cabin C report to the mess hall immediately."

Our summer of servitude lay ahead.

Anna Richards

The four of us (Dexter, Barry, Rodney, and myself) made our way to the center of camp to report to the mess hall. Along the way, I was surprised that none of the campers we were passing by had bothered to talk to us or even offer a wave or head nod of acknowledgment. My guess was that word had gotten around that the kids in The Hole had gotten themselves into hot water already, and it was wise to steer clear of us. It should have bothered me, feeling like the outsider on day one, but overall it just felt natural. Like it was just a regular day in my life back home, a strange familiar comfort in being labeled as 'other' or 'misfit'.

When we finally came up to the mess hall, I could see Deigo and Megan in the shade of a gnarled elm tree just west of the building. Everyone in Camp Alkali's history thought it was the ideal spot to sneak away from the hustle and bustle of camp for some private time with someone. The problem was that everyone knew about the spot, so it wasn't so secret, and it wasn't uncommon to have one couple interrupt another while they were already in the middle of their 'activities'. There was even a rumor that a couple of the councilors were getting hot and heavy by the elm tree one night and that Lester Downs himself caught them in the act, but there was no concrete proof that I'd ever seen.

Diego and Megan looked like they were tangled up with each other, so I figured it'd be best to make ourselves known before we got too close. I shouted out, "Diego, make sure you double-wrap before things go too far!"

Barry joined in. "Yeah! Keep your pants on!"

"Both of you cut it out before someone hears you." Rodney scolded us. He was always looking out for us, even when we didn't have the sense to look out for ourselves.

We watched as Diego pulled himself away from Megan, who appeared to be pleading with him to stay. Megan Drakos was the same age as us but liked to act like she was older and tougher. Her dad was ex-army, and she had four older brothers, and it showed. She had olive skin and deep dark hair; she was short and slightly overweight, but she would beat the living snot out of most boys who dared to cross her. Few people would go out of their way to hit on her, but those that did risked being sucked into her trap, because if she liked you, she was going to fight tooth and nail to never let you go.

"She is crazy about me." Deigo said that once he escaped her grip and made his way over to us, "She asked me if I brought condoms!" He squealed like a toddler.

"Gag me." Dexter jabbed.

"Don't hate the player." Deigo began to say.

"Hate the game." Rodney, Barry, and I finished his sentence with little enthusiasm.

Deigo Conners was a hard kid to figure out—not that he wanted to be figured out. He was an army brat who claimed to have lived in twenty-five states in his short life. His dad was in the Navy, his mom was from Panama, and he was an only child. Everyone knew Deigo for one of three things: his signature messy hair, his terrible one-liners, or the time he went streaking across the docks on a dare in exchange for a girl's number. For the record, the number was fake, but that part of the story rarely got told.

"Just don't go and catch the clap. I can't be associated with reckless dudes who get the clap." Barry smacked Deigo on the back to drive his point home.

A few more jabs were exchanged as we entered the mess hall through its heavy metal doors, where we found Director Downs waiting for us. No pleasantries were exchanged; he got straight to business and wasn't in the mood to have a discussion about it. He told us that the camp maintenance lead, someone he referred to only as Mr. White, was fixing something on the camp generators and couldn't be bothered with us, so we were being assigned kitchen duty. We groaned in disapproval, and he reminded us that it was better than cleaning outhouses, so we stopped whining. A short peppy woman with a head of thinning hair was introduced to us as Mrs. Leaver, and we were told to do everything she said without question.

"Thank you, Lester." She looked over us for a minute, sizing us up and trying to play her cards right. "Okay then, let's get you boys to work."

Mrs. Leaver gave us the basics of how the kitchen worked, introduced us to a few of the full-time staff, and then assigned us each a job and told us why we got said job. Rodney would be serving food in the line because he had a good face. Diego would be in the prep kitchen, cutting vegetables, because he looked like he talked too much. Barry would be cleaning up tables in the dining room because he looked approachable. Finally, Dexter and I would be washing dishes in the far back because we looked like we could use some quality time. We'd only just met that woman, and she had us pegged better than our own mothers did.

The clock in the kitchen read a quarter to five, and dinner would start at five, so we went straight to our jobs and got started. I hated being stuck cleaning dishes with Dexter, but part of me was happy to not have to face every other camper like the others would. The thought alone made my chest hurt from the embarrassment of it all. Camp was supposed to be a place to get away from myself, and instead, my whole first day was spent being reminded of my past. It was hell.

Dinner kicked off in a hurry, and before we knew it, the kitchen was alive with sound. Timers were going off, staff members were hollering instructions back and forth, a booming chorus of conversations echoed off the wooden walls of the mess hall, amplifying the sound, and of course the constant crashing of dishes. Dexter and I were told more than once, by more than one person, that we were loading the dishes wrong or scrapping the dishes wrong, not that either of us cared much. Once dinner service found its rhythm and we found our footing, we were left alone, trusted by Mrs. Leaver to not get into another fist fight.

After what felt like a small eternity of work, I decided to break the silence and maybe get to the bottom of something. "Why'd you punch me? Right away, you just decked me and then said something about declaring war. Why?"

Dexter didn't answer for a minute; instead, he focused on sorting silverware. I asked if he heard me once, and then he answered. "Because that little stunt you pulled last year got me in real trouble with my old man. I got the ass whooping of a lifetime from him after he heard what happened."

"My mom threatened to send me to live with my grandparents. I think she would have given me up for adoption if Dad had let her."

"Damn. That's cold." Dexter said it with a smirk on his face.

"Not as bad as an ass beating, though." I felt sorry for him—only a bit, but I still did.

"You got that right." He let out a small laugh. "How'd that whole thing even end up going sideways? It seemed like everything that could go wrong did."

How'd it all go wrong? Poor judgment, poor planning, and youthful ignorance. But it was deeper than that. I ignored my gut and dove headfirst into a stupid plan, and to make it all worse, I drug the others with me. They assured me that they had my back, and to their credit, they did. I just wish I had theirs.

"I don't want to talk about it."

"Oh, come on! We're stuck back here; we might as well talk."

I looked around the dish area and guessed we only had three or four loads left, and the dull roar of chattering campers had started to dampen, so I figured we were almost done. "No. We'll be out of here soon."

As if to mock me, one of the kitchen staffers turned the corner with a cart full of cookware and started piling it into the dish area. Dexter chuckled. "You were saying?"

We worked in silence for the rest of the night, despite Dexter's pestering. By the time everything was said and done, Mrs. Leaver let us go free at 10:30, a whole five hours later and a half hour of scrubbing dishes. Our hands were so wrinkled from the dishwater that I worried they'd never recover. My feet hurt, my head hurt, I was exhausted, and all I wanted was sleep. Mrs. Leaver had let the others go earlier when they were finished with their duties, so it was just Dexter and I again on the dark walk back to The Hole.

The night air at camp was the stillest, calmest air you could find on Earth. The only noises were the distant hum of path lights, the quiet conversations of crickets and frogs, and the guilty whispers of the few campers who dared to stay up late. As Dexter and I went along, our footsteps on the gravel path cut through that stillness in a way that felt reckless and even rude.

"Seriously, though, why'd you do it, Eddie?" Dexter dared to ask as we passed the dock closest to our cabin.

"Do what?"

"You know what I mean, man. You were always such a goodie-goodie, and then all of a sudden, bam, you're plotting the greatest prank the camps have ever seen. Why?" He sounded sincere, like the question had been nagging at him.

I knew there wasn't time to tell the whole story, not in the hundred feet we had left to The Hole, so I took a sharp left toward the docks. "Follow me."

He did, but Dexter was still worried about it. "If you shove me in, I'll fucking kill you, Eddie."

"Yeah, yeah, yeah. You ain't worth the trouble."

We went to the edge of the dock and sat on the lone bench that looked out over the water. That night, the water was so still that the night sky was perfectly reflected on its surface. The moon and every accompanying star could be seen in a flawless mirrored pattern. It was the kind of image that you don't appreciate until the details start to become fuzzy.

I cleared my throat before speaking, trying to dispel any sense of nervousness in my voice. "Do you remember her name?"

"The girl who almost drowned?"

I nodded, keeping my eyes on the sky's reflection.

"Anna Richards, right?" He sounded confused.

"Yeah. Anna Richards." The image of her panicked eyes under the surface of the water flashed across my mind. It made me shudder. "She was the reason why."

If I were hard-pressed to explain why I opened up to Dexter that night, I'd guess I'd say that I was tired of holding it in. The whole year that had passed was sprinkled with small but painful reminders of what happened to poor Anna Richards. Mom would throw it in my face when she was mad at me; I'd randomly remember it while passing over the bridge to school, and sometimes I'd see her face in my dreams. No one took the time to talk me through what had happened, so I was left to work it out on my own.

The whole thing started innocently enough; even by modern standards, I had a crush on a girl who didn't know I existed. Anna Richards was a fair-skinned girl with purple hair, fake nose piercings, and a fuck-you attitude that even God would have tip-toed around. Looking back, I wasn't sure what her allure was, but I was smitten with full-blown puppy love, and I might as well have been invisible as far as she was concerned.

The funny thing about being a boy and having a crush on a girl is that you have no idea how to approach the situation. You try talking to them and get tongue-tied. You have a buddy who puts in a good word for you that goes nowhere. You even dare to approach one of her friends for help, who will eventually call you a creep, a loser, or whatever. And of course, talking to an adult about the whole thing is out of the question, because the Lord knows they'll only lecture you about morality issues a, b, or c that they see coming down the road. All of it leads to young men picking strange roads to win over the hearts of the folks who catch their eye.

I tried all avenues and got basically nowhere. Between having Barry act as a wingman and my one conversation with a friend of hers, all I managed to learn was that Anna was into 'bad boys' and I clearly wasn't that. There was no denying that I was an awkward kid who still enjoyed cartoons, even though I also took an interest in things like the Cold War. Eddie Matthews was a nerdy, uncool, and quiet kid that only Rodney, Barry, and Deigo seemed to have figured out. The clear answer to my problem was to show her that I was, at least capable, of being a 'bad boy'.

Maybe I watched too many movies as a kid; maybe I just had an overactive imagination; whatever the reason, I had a hair-brained scheme. In the center of the lake was an oversized water mat that was used for games and general hanging out. It was tied to a series of booeyes that were anchored to the bed of the lake, and of course the lake had its famous lake monster stories to go along with it. With my friends help, we came up with a plan to use an old canoe to make a makeshift monster that would pop out of the water at the same time we'd sink the water mat. Rodney was the real brain behind it all, figuring out what weights and pulleys we'd need and how to get it all to work with the pull of a rope.

"You really did all that; to what swoop in and save the day?" Dexter asked while rubbing his arms to fight the chilling night air.

"Well, yeah, but also take credit. Show that I was capable of being a troublemaker or whatever."

"You know, that might be the dumbest fucking thing I've ever heard."

"I know. I didn't say it made sense now; it was just what made sense then." I watched a far-off ripple distort the surface of the water. "Besides, it might have worked if you hadn't shown up."

Dexter sat in silence for a minute, starting at his feet, then said, "Right. You guys were rowing toward the chaos, and we rammed your canoe."

"Yep. You and whatever group of morons you had with you that year."

"I don't even remember their names. Fuck." He leaned his head back and looked toward the sky.

"You put a hole in our canoe, and we had to abandon it. Everything else worked great. The water mat sank, our fake monster terrified everyone who was on the mat, and everyone started swimming for the shore." I watched another ripple, bigger than the last, slide across the water. "But she had asthma."

Dexter whipped his head down to look at me. "Holy shit, for real?"

I nodded. "That's why she didn't make it. You remember seeing her there, right there." I pointed to a place in the water, maybe six feet from the dock we were sitting on. "She made it that far before she quit. And I just stood on this dock, frozen. I made it back fine, I could have went in after her, but I didn't. I froze."

"We all did. If that counselor hadn't jumped in after her." His words hung in the air for a moment.

"I know." A deep sigh pushed its way out of my lungs. "I know."

"If I'd known..." Dexter began to apologize, which I couldn't stand to hear.

"You would have done the same thing, because you're a prick. It wouldn't have changed anything; because you didn't know she had asthma, you probably would have been worse." I could hear myself yelling, my voice like an earthquake in the stillness of the night. "I don't know why you are the way you are, but I'd be happy to never deal with you again, man."

I wasn't sure if it was anger or guilt that had washed over me, but whatever it was made me miserable, and I wanted the day to be over. Before I could get up and march off two equally jarring things happened. First, something splashed in the lake, something big, causing both of us to look out over the water with a peeled eyes. Second, a flashlight peaked out of the darkness behind us, followed by a deep voice bellowing out.

"What in God's name do you boys think you're doing?"

The Charade Began

I couldn't see who was behind the flashlight; the sudden illumination of the world around me made it even harder to see. Both Dexter and I put our hands above our heads as a sign of surrender, not that it made much sense to do so in that situation. Whoever was shining the flashlight on us began to walk toward us, down the creaking walkway of the dock.

The voice boomed out again. "I said, what are you boys doing?"

"Nothing sir." I blurted out. "We were just talking. That's all, sir. Cross my heart and hope to die; that's the truth."

"You know it's an hour past curfew, don't you?" He asked, a bit softer than before.

Dexter took a step closer and spoke. "We were working in the kitchen; they didn't let us out until after curfew. The only reason we stopped her was to unwind for a bit before heading back to The Hole."

"Aw, shit." The mystery man flicked his flashlight off. "You two are with me then. That's just fucking dandy."

After a few moments of my eyes adjusting, I could make out the face of the stranger. He was in his late twenties at the most, with an unflattering neck beard, deep-set beady eyes, and bright blonde hair. He was wearing some sort of jumpsuit, with the sleeves rolled up, clearly unbothered by the chilly temperatures of the summer night, and a name was stitched on them that read 'Levi' with bright red string. His expression was something between annoyed and exhausted, with a dash of wishing he could be elsewhere.

"So you're Dexter and Edward then? I wondered where you wandered off too." He started walking back to the shore and motioned for us to follow. "Let's get to bed; tomorrow is going to be busy as hell."

Dexter and I did as we were told and followed suit. The Hole wasn't far from the dock, so we were inside and in our bunks in only a few minutes. The others were already asleep, with Barry snoring like a rhino with a sinus infection, and our newly appointed babysitter Levi took the bunk closest to the door. I didn't expect sleep to come easy, especially after reliving the near murder of Anna Richards, but the work in the mess hall drained me. Sleep and I usually wrestled, but that night I didn't stand a chance.

The next morning, we were woken up by the sound of a cowbell clamoring inside our cabin. My eyes shut open, and I immediately shot up, causing me to hit my forehead into the unoccupied bunk above me. All I could manage to do was roll to the floor and then jump up, only wearing my boxers, looking for some sign of danger. All I found was the stranger from the dock, banging away at a cowbell by the door.

"Rise and shine, shit stains, there's work to be done." He shouted with a grin cut across his face.

Rodney and Diego jumped out of bed, looking just as bewildered as I was. Dexter pulled the covers over his head, and Barry kept on sleeping, completely unbothered by the noise. It was still dark out, and the only sound I could hear other than the cowbell banging was the panicked rustling of whatever lived in the walls of The Hole, who must have also been startled awake just like us.

"What the hell, dude?" Dexter groaned from his bunk.

"It's time to get to work, dude, that's what." He tossed the cowbell into his bunk and put his hands on his hips. "Let's get a few things straight now. First, I'm stuck with you, and you're stuck with me, so do what you're told, and our time together will fly by. Second, only do what I say as I say it. I don't need anyone losing a finger because they thought they knew better." As he spoke, his voice swung up and down, and a bit of sweat formed on his forehead. He was fronting. "Lastly, you may call me Mr. White. Sounds good?"

Rodney must have seen what I saw because he went right for the soft spot. "Sir, does your mama call you Mr. White?"

"Well, no." He stuttered

"How about your dad or your siblings?" Rodney took a step toward him, and he took a step back.

"No, but that's not the point. I..."

"Your friends call you Mr. White, sir?" Rodney copied the hands on the hips' power stance.

He paused for a moment and swallowed hard. "No."

"It's Levi, right?" I asked, feeling a bit smug. "Your name is Levi?"

A shallow sigh slipped from his mouth. "Yes, it's Levi."

"Alright then, Levi, do you mind explaining what exactly is going on here?" Rodney had taken control of the conversation. It was one of the coolest things I'd ever seen—a teenager walking an adult into a corner and taking their keys.

Levi sat on his bunk, looking partially defeated and partially annoyed. "Listen, guys, the director gave me very clear orders that I was supposed to keep you in line. It's my first year here, and the only reason I'm here is because it was supposed to be easy. I didn't expect to have to watch a bunch of kids."

I dug a pair of shorts out of my bag and slipped them on before asking, "So why did the tough guy act? Just let us lay low, and we'll stay out of your way, yeah?"

He shook his head in a short, quick manner. "No, I can't do it. Director Downs said he'd be checking in every day and that he wanted to see you guys breaking a sweat. Whatever you did, he ain't happy about it."

At that point, Dexter had finally dug his way out of his sheets and into the conversation. "What's the plan, then, maintenance man? Clean outhouses and fix signs. All for what, helping you keep your job?"

Dexter had a point, so I asked, "What do we get out of this?"

Levi looked up at us, probably wondering how he ended up in negotiations with campers, and sputtered, "To stay at camp?"

"Not enough." Deigo barked and sounded a bit too excited. "We ain't going to spend all our time with you and being trapped in here and fixing stuff. No way, dude, we need something extra."

"Guys, I need this job." Levi stood up, and even though he was taller than everyone but Rodney, he clearly felt like the smallest one there. "I can't just let you do whatever you want."

He made a point, not that any of us were going to say it out loud, but we did have the upper hand then. Director Downs would come around looking for proof that we were being punished, and Levi apparently couldn't afford to disappoint him. If we were caught slacking off, we'd probably get sent home, which would only cause us to get in even deeper shit with parents. It was a rock and a hard place, and we needed a middle ground.

"Fine." I chimed in. "We'll help you with the easy stuff, just enough to get Downs off our backs and yours. Outside of that, though, you stay out of our way, and we stay out of yours. Sound good?"

"Well, kinda. Here's the thing: I'm supposed to look after you guys, so if we do this, we have to act like I'm in charge." Levi started to nervously wring his hands. "We'll have to eat our meals together; Downs made that clear, and I'm supposed to sleep here in the cabin. But I guess if we do enough to keep Downs happy, you could slip off now and then. If you get caught though, you're on your own."

"Eddie, are you sure about this?" Diego asked.

"Think about it. We'll be free to do as we please. No rigid schedule, no lame group games, and no counselors. When all those kids are stuck out in the heat for some stupid relay race or something, we can hang out in the AC or go for a swim. Hell, we could even try to find the outlaw hideout; everyone talks about it."

There was a pause while the others mulled it over until Rodney finally spoke for us. "Alright, Mr. White, throw in zero kitchen duty, and we got us a deal?"

Levi and Rodney shook hands, and the charade began.

We learned quickly about the storyline that we were supposed to perform each day to keep Downs happy. The day would start at a quarter past six in the morning, so we could eat breakfast with the staff. After that, we'd have a morning project in full view of the camp to show us being good boys serving their time, followed by a sack lunch we'd pick up at the mess hall, and finally a midday project also in full view of the camp. Levi said we'd have the option to eat dinner with the rest of the camp and that he'd do what he could to keep us off kitchen duty. The five of us would be free to do as we pleased in between tasks as long as we stayed out of sight and didn't draw attention to ourselves.

The first part of the day was dull. After we managed to wake Barry from his dead man's slumber, we all got dressed and followed Levi to breakfast, where we sat at a table alone while the camp staff ate and whispered about us from across the room. Once we finished up there, we went with Levi to the docks to clean out canoes and check for loose deck boards. When that was done, Diego snuck off to see Megan, Dexter went off to god knows where, and Rodney, Barry, and I went back to The Hole to recoup some of the sleep we lost from waking up early.

Eventually, Diego came bursting through the door of our cabin, waking us up with a sing-songy voice. "Your boy is going to get laid." Our groans of disapproval didn't satisfy his need for a response, so he repeated himself. "I said, Your boy is going to have sex!"

"Man, shut the fuck up." Rodney threw a pillow at him.

"Yeah, dude, just chill out a bit. Alright?" Barry agreed.

"I'm serious, guys! She says she wants me; like, she can't even keep her hands off me." Diego kicked his sneakers off and sat on one of the bunks.

"No offense, Diego, but I don't want to hear about you trying to fuck Manic Megan." I quipped, pulling myself out of bed. "Besides, we're supposed to be keeping a low profile, remember?"

"Manic Megan, that's going to stick." Barry laughed.

"Not cool, guys. Not cool." Diego crossed his arms in protest.

"Seriously though, man, what the hell are you going on about?" I dared to ask.

"She said she wants me to be her first. We were hanging out in her cabin, you know, getting handsy, and she just said it flat out. And she's serious about it, guys; I know she is. I just got to find a spot."

Rodney got up, walked across the room, sat next to Diego, and put his arm around him. "You're telling us that you want to pop a girl's cherry, who you barely know, somewhere in the woods?" Diego shrugged sheepishly. "The boy's crazy. Simple as that."

Diego pulled his arm off and stood up. "What's so wrong with being in love, huh?"

"Oh, so it's love now, is it?" Barry asked with another laugh.

The debate about Diego's sex life, or lack thereof, was cut short by Dexter busting into the room. His face was red, probably sunburnt, and drenched in sweat. He looked like he'd just hiked across the desert or zig-zagged his way across a World War II battlefield.

Dexter rested his hands on his knees and spoke in a raspy, out-of-breath voice. "You guys aren't going to believe what I fucking found."

Eviction

"You guys just have to trust me. I found it! You got to see it."
Dexter said, trying to convince us to follow him to lord knows
where.

"Why would we follow you blindly into no man's land?
You and your band of cretins have had it out for us since the
fourth grade." Barry was usually the easygoing one, but even he
knew something was off.

"To be fair, he doesn't have his groupies with him this year."
Rodney added. He stood by the door with his arms crossed,
making a point to show Dexter that he was watching him.

"Seriously? You guys trust me that little." Dexter protested,
still slightly out of breath.

"Are you surprised?" I asked.

Diego headed toward the door with his mind on other
things. "Listen, if we're done here, I'm going to go find my lady
friend."

In an incredible streak of bad luck, Levi happened to pull
the door open at that moment, causing Diego to miss the
handle and stummble. He was carrying two grocery bags filled
with small brown sacks and was wearing a perplexed look on
his face. "Lady friend? Did I hear that right?"

I'd never seen Diego beam with pride like he did that day.
He'd convinced himself that to be a man, you had to take a
woman all the way. In an old-school, turn-of-the-century kind

of mindset, I suppose he was right, but even by the standards of the early 2000's, he was being ridiculous. Still, in that moment, he was proud, feeling that he was on the threshold of greatness.

"Yes, sir, you heard right. Now if you'll excuse me, I have better things to be doing." He went for the door, but Levi blocked it.

"That wasn't in the deal, guys. Please don't tell me you're sneaking into the girl's cabin." Levi didn't sound panicky, but he didn't sound calm either.

Diego looked at him with guilt written all over his face. "Define 'sneak in.'"

Levi dropped his head and dropped the grocery bags on the floor. "Here. You guys forgot to show up to collect your lunch. I was able to cover for you. Downs aksed why you weren't there, so you got a job you need to do now."

"Nothing too gross, right?" Barry asked, grabbing a sack lunch from the bag.

"No, it's gross. But it's all I could think of." Levi took a seat on his bunk and kicked his boots off.

"Well?" I dared to ask. "What is it?"

"I told him you guys were going to clean out under Cabin E. They've got something building a nest under there, and it's making the girls feel unsafe. Downs was happy to hear it and told me to wish you boys luck."

Diego's face beamed. "Hey, that's Megan's cabin. This could work out."

"Keep your pants on, lover boy. You're stuck with us until the job's done. That was the deal." Rodney reminded him.

"Fine." Diego scoffed and grabbed himself a lunch.

Levi told us the sack lunches were the same every day and warned us that complaining would only get us in trouble with the kitchen staff. PB&J sandwich, an apple, a small bag of trail mix, a bottle of water, and whatever dessert was leftover from the last dinner service (usually some kind of bar). We were expected to go pick up our lunches with the rest of the support staff before the mess hall opened to campers. He, again, made it clear that Director Downs would be on the lookout for us the next day, and if we were smart, we'd remember to show up.

We sat and ate in our bunks, which probably encouraged the ant problem we already had, and shot the shit about all the things we hadn't had the time to catch up on yet. Rodney got grilled for shaving his budding afro from the year before, and though he maintained that his father made him do it because he got into a fight at school, the rest of us were convinced that he also was slightly embarrassed by it. Barry was given a hard time getting caught with vodka in his backpack again, which he insisted he would have gotten away with if his sister wasn't a narc. Diego tried to talk about Megan more, but we demanded an update on the shoplifting accident he'd written us about over the summer, and he reluctantly told us how his mom was able to get the charges dropped. The three of them poked and prodded at me about how life had been, but I kept my walls up; I'd gotten good at that.

I wanted to tell them that Mom made me start seeing a counselor after what had happened with Anna Richards. I wanted to tell them that the counselor made me relive things I didn't want to. I wanted to tell them that my father started spending too much time at work. I wanted to tell them that a man I didn't know started calling the house and asking to speak with my mom every night my dad stayed at the office late. I wanted to feel like I could tell them. Instead, they got updates on crushes that went nowhere, teachers that I felt had it out for me, and how my dog was getting old.

The whole time we talked, no one asked Dexter for his input, and none of us bothered to ask him what was new in his life because we didn't care. I watched him, though, as he sat in his bunk staring at the floor, chewing slowly as he did. We'd spent enough summers together that I knew his face well enough, so I could tell when he was angry, embarrassed, or disinterested. But that day, he looked like he was stewing on something, like he was trying to convince himself of something he didn't believe.

"Alright, that's enough." Levi rolled out of his bunk and slipped his boots on. "Time to go find out what's living under that cabin.

The five of us did as we were told, slipped our shoes on, and followed Levi. We stopped at the maintenance shed first and grabbed everything Levi told us we'd need, then made our way down to Cabin E. The whole way there, we passed groups of kids engaging in the usual summer camp fair. A group of girls building birdhouses snickered and whispered as we passed. A pack of boys playing touch football in the clearing openly pointed and mocked. Word had gotten around, and despite what Rodney had hoped, we were not the victors.

Levi had us bring rope, bear spray, two brooms, a hose, and a net on a pole (the kind that cartoon characters used to catch butterflies, just much larger). None of us were sure how we were going to use those tools, but we assumed Levi had a plan. We quickly learned that he didn't.

"Well, get to it." He said that and pointed to the cabin.

Each of the six cabins was raised off the ground and built on slowly decaying log footings, so there was a three to four foot gap under each cabin, and it wasn't uncommon for small animals to make a home under there. Usually, it was a rabbit, maybe a raccoon, or a fox. But when your luck turned sour, you'd get a skunk. That was our fear.

"What?" I didn't ask as much as I proclaimed. "We don't know what we're doing. You're the maintenance guy."

"It's easy. Just crawl under there and, uh, evict whatever's down there. Easy peasy."

Dexter spoke up first. "I am not going down there."

"Me either." Diego agreed.

"Same." Rodney said, taking two steps back.

"That leaves you two, then." Levi said, slapping Barry and me on the back.

Barry and I each grabbed a broom, and he grabbed the bear spray before getting onto our stomachs and crawling under the cabin. We devised a plan where Rodney waited outside with a net, Dexter was on standby with the rope, and Diego was being waiting with the hose. Each on a different side of the cabin to hopefully catch whatever we scared out. It was a terrible plan, but it was our plan, so we went with it.

"Do you think we're going to find anything cool?" Barry asked as we crawled.

"Like what?" I asked as a cobweb attached itself to my face.

"I don't know. Some creepy camp monster or something."

"The only monster they say is here is the one in the lake."

"Fair." He sounded defeated.

The first few feet we crawled, all we found were cobwebs, old leaves, and more cobwebs.

"Nothing yet." I hollered out.

"Just keep looking." Levi hollered back. "You're bound to come across something."

We went a few more feet when we noticed a hole near one of the footings. It was about the size of a football and had some kind of footprint scattered around it. I wasn't much of an outdoorsy kid, but even I knew that wasn't a good sign.

"Bet you it's a fox." Barry chimed before yelling at the other. "We got something. It's a hole."

"What kind of hole?" Diego asked, sounding a bit shaky. He'd always been timid around animals, even small ones; something about a dog bite as a kid. When I found that out I gave him hell on year about being afraid of rabbits. He hated me for that.

"I don't know. An animal hole?" Barry answered while rolling his eyes.

We crawled closer to the hole and could hear something rustling inside.

"Do foxes bite people?" I dared to ask, afraid I already knew the answer.

We didn't have to wait to find out. Out of the darkness of the den, two skunks came out, hissing and running for us. The details of what happened next are fuzzy at best and likely out of order. I remember the smell first, then screaming, followed by more screaming farther off. After that, I remember hitting my head, more screaming, and, of course, a more terrible smell. Needless to say, we did evict the skunks from their den but paid a hefty sum for our efforts.

As it turned out, there was a protocol in place for when someone was attacked by a skunk. First, you'd be stripped of your clothes down to your underwear behind the mess hall, and then Nurse Linda would hand you a bucket that contained a mixture of hydrogen peroxide, baking soda, and dish soap. You'd be instructed to scrub yourself down in every nook and cranny until you were completely covered. Once that was done, you'd be hosed off with an actual hose by a member of the staff. While that was happening, someone else would go burn your clothes, which they'd send a check home for, and anyone who happened to be walking by could see.

I'm not sure which was worse, the pointing and laughing as we walked to the mess hall to have all that done or the small crowd that formed to watch us be put on display. Both situations sucked, both situations hurt, and both situations made me wish they'd just banned me the year before instead of allowing me to return, only to make my life hell.

Once it was all said and done, we were given towels and sent back to The Hole. Director Downs told us we could have the rest of the day off but demanded that Levi meet with him in his office and didn't even allow him to get dressed. As a kid who's just starting to adapt to the behaviors that are expected of them going into adolescence, public humiliation can either make or break you, and we were all pretty busted up, except Dexter.

We'd barely gotten into dry clothes when he said, "Come on. I need to show you guys what I saw earlier."

"What the hell are you talking about? I ain't going back out there. Everybody was pointing my thing." Diego said, sounding like a dog with his tail between his legs. "I can't face anyone right now."

Barry was more concerned with his stomach than Diego's pride. "What about dinner?"

Dexter's tone shifted to one I'd been familiar with: frustrated and on the edge of violence. "Really, Barry? You want to go eat with all the kids that laughed at us?"

"Well, I guess not."

"Right. Besides, Levi's probably getting canned right now for letting a bunch of kids deal with wild animals. Now's our chance to get out of here for a while."

Rodney leaned in front of the door. "Where exactly are we going?"

"To the edge of the property, on the far side of the lake. I saw, well, you'll see what I saw." Dexter said, inching closer to punching someone.

I didn't trust Dexter, that was for damn sure, but I also had no reason to fear him in that situation. My friends and I outnumbered him four to one, and without his gang of enforcers, he seemed a lot less bold. I'm not sure what came over me; maybe I wanted to avoid any violence, or maybe I just wanted to get as far away from the scene of my humiliation as possible, but I backed him up.

"Let's give him a shot." I said, motioning for Rodney to back away from the door. "It's not like he's going to murder us. Right Dexter?"

He didn't answer before he stepped out the door.

The James Riley Gang

Only three things could be heard that night: the mating calls of bullfrogs, the dull rumble of campers packed into the far-off mess hall, and the constant drone of multiple AC units fighting like hell to ward off the sticky July air. Rodney, Barry, Diego, and I all followed Dexter to the edge of the camp's border and onto a thin path that weaved along the forest floor. The sun was in its final stages of daylight, painting the horizon hues of purple and orange and barely illuminating the path we were traveling along. It would be dark in a matter of moments, but none of us dared mention that we forgot flashlights.

"You mind telling us where we're going exactly?" I asked.

"Just hold your fucking horses. Jesus Christ." Dexter quipped, not bothering to look back at me, keeping his eyes on the fading trail in front of him.

Rodney leaned close to me. "If he tries anything, we leave him here, yeah?"

"Yeah." I agreed. "No questions asked." As far as I was concerned it would be a fitting fate for my long time rival.

A few feet later, the trail we'd been following had vanished, and we found ourselves in a small clearing on a hilltop. The last flares of sunlight danced off the lake below us, and even at that young age, the beauty struck me. Down in the camp, surrounded by decaying buildings and the social pressures of peers, the beauty that surrounded us got overlooked.

"This is it." Dexter said, stepping further into the clearing.

Diego looked confused and a bit annoyed. "What? You drug us out of here for a sunset?"

"Not the sunset, you moron! That." He pointed out the water below.

As the long shadows of the forest began to stretch across the lake, taking the shine away from its waves, a small black speck stood out. An island, or at least nature's minimum requirement for an island, poked out from the whitecaps at the far end of the lake. I figured from the shores of the camp you'd be hard-pressed to see it, but still, it was there.

"An island?" Barry asked. "You think it's always been there?"

Rodney punched him on the shoulder. "Yes! God, Barry, you worry me."

"What's the big deal?" Diego asked, squinting as he looked. "You found an island, bravo. Can we go now?"

Serving as Dexter's annual punching bag and prey was a shitty existence, but it had one upside: I understood how his mind worked better than anyone else around us. It wasn't just some island; it was the island that all the stories we'd heard as campers talked about. Dexter was betting that this island, barely poking out of the water, was the hiding place of the James Riley gang.

There were three tall tales that made the rounds every year at camp. First was the Alkali Lake Monster that supposedly lurked in the deepest part of the lake, snatching up unsuspecting campers who strayed a tad too far from shore. Second were the cement tubes laid at the bottom of the lake, filled with uranium, that the government dumped after World

War Two. And the final was the hideout of famed outlaw James Riley which, as rumor has it, was lost under the tide as the water in the lake rose over the years.

The story claimed that James Riley was a horsethief with a mean streak from birth. Supposedly, he first killed a man when he was fourteen years old while stealing a horse, and his reputation grew from there. The story said he kept a posse of men just as brutal as him and that they stored the profits from their crimes somewhere near Lake Alkali. According to the ghost stories, his spirit still haunted the old hideout, kept watch over his loot, and scared off anyone who dared to get too close.

"You've got to be fucking joking. You think the hideout is down there?" I asked, pointing at the speck below.

"Well, yeah, isn't it obvious?" Dexter sounded offended.

"Wait, wait, wait." Rodney waved his hands back and forth in protest. "You drug us all the way out here because of some campfire story?"

"You mean the outlaw hideout? That's a myth." Diego asked, looking as angry as Rodney did.

"I don't know. I always thought it was a cool story." Barry added, causing each of us to look at him in disbelief.

Dexter turned to the group, his face steeled against our doubts, and said, "Listen. I'm not saying there is, or isn't, anything on that island. All I'm saying is that there is an island. Think about it. We have all this downtime now that we're stuck on maintenance duty, why not use it to go on an adventure?"

"Why? For all we know, it's just a rock sticking out of the water." I surprised myself with how angry I sounded.

"Because it beats napping in the hole while Diego tries to get the clap." Dexter laughed a bit at the end of his answer. I didn't blame him.

"Hey!" Diego protested, which caused the rest of us to laugh too.

I let out a sigh and shook my head a bit, not believing what I was going to say. "Alright, fine. I'm in."

The others agreed in their own way, and we started to discuss what we'd need just as the sun tucked behind the tree line. As the darkness took over and we all finally admitted we'd forgotten a flashlight, the unease of a dark forest started to dawn on us. None of us would dare say we were scared, but we all agreed that the air suddenly felt off.

Barry had a flip phone, a fairly impressive feat in 2002, and was elected to lead us back to camp using its dim screen as a minimal source of light. Rodney followed him, then Dexter and Diego, with myself in the rear. It wasn't a position I enjoyed being in.

We did find our way back to the trail, though it took longer than I felt it should have. Chatter was kept to a minimum as we went along, mostly just relaying messages to watch our step or asking if we heard some sound. No one dared to speak above a whisper, and each step we took had intention behind it.

The path we took followed the edge of a drop-off that plummeted straight into the lake. As we descended the hill, the sound of the waves against the wall of earth began to grow louder. Darkness had hold of the forest, but the moonlight illuminated the lake's surface and gave off a soft glow, which let us see whitecaps forming with the strong winds of the night. Under different circumstances, it would have been quite the sight, but something about that night made it look ominous. Like the lake itself was enraged and looking for violence.

Dexter eventually stopped, causing Diego and me to bump into him. "Do you guys see that? By the opposite shore?" His voice shook a bit as he spoke.

"I don't see anything." Diego whispered.

My eyes searched the surface of the water, looking for anything unusual. At first, I didn't see anything—no boats, no floating objects, no oddly shaped driftwood—nothing on the surface looked out of place. Then my eyes were drawn to a color that didn't belong, glowing under the water, seemingly bobbing along with the whitecaps.

"You mean those green things?" I asked, speaking louder than anyone had so far on the walk back. "Under the water, right?"

Dexter only nodded.

The others looked out to the lake, and eventually, they all saw it too. No one had a theory on what it was or even what it could be; we just agreed that it felt wrong. And something else was wrong too; the strange feeling in the air had somehow grown into a sense of budding dread.

"Do you guys hear ringing? Or maybe buzzing?" Barry asked, his eyes still fixed on the water.

Rodney pulled his stare off the lake and cupped over his ears. "Yeah, I do. It feels like I sat too close to the Fourth of July display."

I heard it too—a high-pitched buzz that was growing louder and louder with every second. My vision started to darken at the edges, and I could feel my heart rate start to increase. Looking over at the others, they were all either covering their ears or whining in pain, but I just stood there, frozen. Time became tricky to pin down, and it felt like we stood there for ages like that until we snapped out of it. All at the same time.

There was a crack and the distant sound of a twig snapping underfoot, somewhere up the path. Each of us instantly had our faculties back—no ringing, no frozen feeling, just a sudden fear of whatever made that noise. None of us dared to speak until we saw a figure appear on the path ahead of us.

"What the fuck is that?" Diego asked, his voice suddenly raspy.

Rodney leaned forward, trying to get a better look at it. "I don't know, but whatever it is, it can't be good."

"What do we do?" Barry asked, still holding his phone up for light.

I'd learned you had two choices when you faced a problem: either hope it went away or do something about it. I found that waiting for them to go away rarely worked. "Rush it."

"What?" Barry sounded shocked.

"We rush it and we go straight at it as fast as we can. Don't move out of the way, just run. It'll get scarred off, whatever it is." I had no reason to be, but I was sure.

"He's right." Rodney agreed. "On three. One, two, three."

Each of us let out a yell and dashed down the path to the figure. Our screams and footsteps echoed throughout the woods and revered back to our ears, amplifying the noise of the whole ordeal. I can't say for sure what the others were feeling in that moment, but I felt nothing; it was like autopilot had kicked in, and running toward an unknown figure in the woods was the natural thing to do.

We made it close to the stranger, maybe five feet away, when a beam of light ran into our faces, causing all of us to stop in our tracks.

"What in God's name are you guys doing?" Levi's voice rang out from behind the light. "I've been looking everywhere for you!"

There was a moment of silence while we got our sight back and calmed our nerves before he asked again, "What were you guys doing out here?"

"Dexter wanted to show us something up on that hill." Barry answered, rubbing his eyes, trying to dispel the floaters in his vision.

Levi rubbed his furrowed brow. "Big clearing at the top, yeah?"

"How'd you know?" Rodney asked.

"It's the old make-out spot that campers used in the nineties." He flashed his flashlight past up along the trail. "I'm surprised this trail is still here."

"A make-out spot? Huh." Diego said, sounding too interested.

Levi shined the flashlight in his face. "Don't get any ideas, lover boy. Besides, you guys really can't go this far outside the camp. Weird shit happens in these woods all the time."

"Oh, come on," Rodney said, sounding half playful and half serious. "You don't believe in those ghost stories, do you?"

"Ghosts? No." Levi pointed his flashlight on the lake. "It's the lake that freaks me out. Weird shit lives in the deep end, I'm telling you. When I was a kid, we'd come out here, and I swear I'd see these big green eyes stare up at us as we canoed."

I pointed to the distant shore, still dimly lit under the moonlight. "Like those ones?"

Levi looked, and his face went flat and pale. The others looked too, trying to match his stare, and found the green eyes, still bobbing with the whitecaps, glaring back at us. In an instant, I watched the eyes disappear as they sank deeper into the water, followed by something huge and dark rippling across the lake surface, creating new waves. My mouth wanted to ask what had happened, but before I could speak, a deep groan rolled up the lake's shore and into the woods, and Levi's face came back to life.

"We need to run. You hear me? Run!" He bolted down the trail toward camp.

None of us asked questions; we just did as we were told. The same autopilot that told me to rush Levi now told me to run and not stop running until I was back at the cabin. All the while, the sound of massive waves roared from the lake. The winds blew harder and harder, and the sound of my own labored breathing filled my head. I couldn't make heads or tails of what was happening around me; it was like a fog had settled on my mind.

At one point, Rodney tripped and fell to his hands and knees. Diego and Dexter bolted past him without a word, but I stopped and tried to help him up. Rodney was taller and heavier than I was, and he wasn't budging. He just stared out into the raging water, mouthing the words 'leave me' again and again. It wasn't until a clap of thunder rang out that he snapped out of his daze and started moving again. We didn't stop running until we were back in The Hole, gasping for air and answers.

In between heavy breaths, I asked, "Levi, what the fuck was that?"

I Could Just Quit, Ya Know?

"You don't expect us to believe that, do you? That's insane! Even for a camp monster, it's over the top. I mean, a lake monster in the middle of Nebraska? Is it supposed to be like a dragon, or a dinosaur or something?" Diego was spitting mad, waving his hands above his head while he spoke.

It didn't take much prodding for Levi to tell us everything he knew. He'd been a camper himself when he was young, and in those days, the legend of the Alkali Lake Monster was very much alive and used as a scare tactic to keep campers from swimming out too far. They used to sell shirts and buttons with the monster image, and it even served as a kind of mascot.

The story was that the monster used to be your average salamander or lizard until it was exposed to something. In 1948, Lake Alkali was smaller—much smaller than its current size—until the federal government announced a project to increase its capacity. Newspapers at the time claimed it was an effort to have more available water near the Nebraska National Forest in case of wildfires, but other theories quickly arose. Prominent among them was that the government had dumped a truckload of cement containers loaded with nuclear waste, which mutated some poor, unsuspecting amphibian into the monster the area had come to know.

"I'm not saying it makes sense, alright? Those are just the stories!" Levi barked back, clearly growing irritated with Diego's protesting.

Barry, unbothered by the conflict, chimed in. "It actually makes some sense. I mean, in like a comic book kind of way, you know what I mean?"

"No! I just got spooked. It was just the storm rising up." Levi said this before crawling into his bunk and pulling the covers over his head. "It's late. Let's just get some sleep, and we can deal with it in the morning."

"What about the eyes, man?" Dexter asked, sounding like his mind was still back there, overlooking the water. "You saw the eyes, didn't you?"

"I did." Rodney answers in such a matter-of-fact manner that Deigo didn't bother to challenge him.

"You boys are just tired. Goodnight." Levi reached for the wall and switched the lights off.

I'm not sure any of us slept well that night, if at all, but if someone were to stumble into our cabin with the lights off, they'd think it was abandoned. None of us said another word or even bothered to readjust on our stiff mattress. The only sounds that night were the winds brushing against the siding, the mystery creature stirring in the wall, and the raging whitecaps of the lake in the distance. Though I wondered if they were really whitecaps or maybe waves created from the strong movements of some overgrown lizard with bright green eyes,.

If I slept, it was brief, and if I dreamed, the memories escaped me.

Morning dawned in the fashion you came to expect at camp—too quickly with an early heat wave—and for some reason, I woke up before Dexter or my friends. I noticed that Levi wasn't in his bunk and that the cabin door was cracked open. The air in The Hole was thick, and the smell of adolescent body odor had started to set into every fiber of the place, so I figured I'd step out for some fresh air. I changed my clothes and stepped outside, where I found him sitting on the steps, smoking a cigarette.

"Morning." He grunted while cheap smoke billowed around his head. "The others up?"

I shivered as my body adjusted from the dark chill of the cabin to the sudden heat of the Nebraskan summer sun. "Nope. Just me. What time is it anyway?"

He checked his watch and flicked ash from his cigarette. "Quater before six."

"Damn."

"Yeah. I didn't mean to get up this early, it just sort of happened." He took another draw.

"Same. I don't know what woke me up, but I figured I was already up." I took a seat next to him on the steps.

Whatever brand of cigarettes he smoked smelled much cheaper than the cancer sticks my mother kept in her purse. I was around the age when a lot of kids in my school had started to get into smoking or drinking, always stealing crumbs of vice from their parent's or grandparents' supply. Not me, though, not because I took some moral high ground against it; my reasons were much more personal. Rooted in the simple idea that I didn't want to be like my parents, my mother smoked like a chimney and my father drank like a fish.

"What's bugging you?" I asked, squinting as I looked out at the lake. Now calm and almost serious-looking.

Levi side-eyed me and frowned. "What makes you think something is bugging me?"

"Your shoulders are stiff and drawn back, and that usually means that someone is tense. It could be from the shitty mattress, but I'm willing to bet it's not." I'd always been good at reading people.

Levi nodded and flicked his cigarette into a puddle on the path that led to our cabin. "Yeah, well, I have a lot to be tense about."

"Want to talk about it?"

He raised an eyebrow. "With you?"

I shrugged and batted a mosquito away from my face. "Got anyone else to talk to?"

His face scrunched up while he thought before letting out a sigh. "I just really need this job. Between the skunk problem and you guys sneaking off last night, I'm just worried I'll lose it."

"Why's that?" I knew it was a stupid question to ask, but it was the only one I could think of.

"Because Downs was already on my ass about being a bad maintenance guy, now I'm a bad maintenance guy and a bad counselor." He put his face in his palms.

Part of me wanted to pat him on the back, but another part told me that was a bad idea. "To be fair, I don't think Downs said anything to me about you being our counselor."

He didn't respond; he only dropped his head in shame.

"Besides, why do you care what Downs thinks? Worst-case scenario: you get canned and find another job, right?" That statement showed how little I knew about the world then. Despite thinking I knew everything I needed to know,.

Levi let out a sarcastic laugh that was just loud enough to scare off a small flock of sparrows that were foraging for scraps on the beach. "If only, if only. Nah, kid, I'm homeless. That's the whole reason I took this job—to have a place to stay. I saw a posting on Craigslist and figured I already knew the place, so it couldn't be that bad. Man, was I wrong?"

"Damn." I squirmed where I sat while I searched for words that felt appropriate. "So, are you homeless because of the war or something? Like those vets on the news?"

"What? No." He stood up and looked at me puzzled. "How old do you think I am?"

I wasn't sure, but to be fair, when you're a kid, everyone either looks thirty, sixty, or a hundred. "Thirty?"

"Thirty? I'm twenty-two!" Levi sat back down and put his hands in his face. "I should have left after that first week. This was a bad idea. I've got no idea what I'm doing, and now I let you guys paint me into a corner. Downs could have fired me last night and I swore he was going to when he pulled me to his office, but no. He just had to say he believed in me. Ugh." He pulled his hands from his face and groaned. "If it wasn't for her, I could just quit, you know? Up and leave. But she's here."

In my home life, I'd gotten used to adults oversharing with me. I can't say for sure why it happened, but it did. Whether it was Mom complaining about Dad, my grandparents complaining about my parents, or my older cousins complaining about my aunts and uncles, there was something about having a young Eddie in the room that made people feel safe telling me things I had no business knowing. To be fair, over the years I realized this did a number on me, but while it was happening, I got quite good at follow-up questions. Why? I hated having half the story.

"She? Got yourself a lady friend, Levi?" I tried to not sound smug.

He looked at the ground sheepishly. "Yeah. Olivia Burrell. We both came here as kids, and when I started working here, I ran into her again. She's a counselor in one of the girl cabins." A goofy smile plastered itself on his face. "She remembered me, and we hit it off. But then she asked what I'd been doing with my life, and I didn't have the heart to tell her..."

His voice trailed off. "Tell her what?"

"That my music career didn't pan out and that my parents wouldn't let me move back in, so now I work at camp so I have a place to sleep." He let out a sigh. "That's a surefire way to make a girl think you're a loser."

"I'd say." Dexter's voice came from behind us.

Levi and I both spun around in a hurry, and I almost toppled back. Dexter, Barry, Diego, and Rodney were all standing in the doorway, staring at us from the other side of the screen door. Their expressions were hard to read, but a common look of pity seemed to loom on all of their faces.

"How long have you been standing there?" Levi asked, sounding a bit huffed.

"Long enough to know that Diego isn't the only one in The Hole that got bit by the love bug." Rodney quipped with a huge smile, holding back laughter.

"Man, shut the fuck up." Diego shoved him. "The heart is a powerful thing; it ain't my fault you haven't experienced love yet."

"You and Manic Megan are not in love." Rodney shoved him back.

I let out a stifled laugh, proud that my nickname had stuck, which got Diego to switch his anger toward me.

"The fuck are you laughing at, Eddie?" He tried to push past the other to get to me.

"Alright, alright, enough!" Levi put himself between me and the screen door. "We're going to be late for breakfast, and like it or not, Director Downs is still expecting us to work."

"Even after the skunk spray?" Barry asked, sounding a bit traumatized from the prior day's events.

"Especially after the skunk spray."

Levi marched us down to breakfast with minimal fuss from us. We found ourselves in the position of mutually assured destruction; he could rat us out to Downs for sneaking out, and we could rat him out by exposing our little deal, so it made sense in the meantime to play nice. Partly to save our own skins from being shipped back home to vengeful parents, but mostly to try and salvage the autonomy we'd already negotiated with him.

Breakfast was pancakes, scrambled eggs, sausage, and a hearty dose of mockery from the kitchen staff. The six of us sat at a table in the corner of the mess hall while the kitchen crew snickered amongst themselves and pointed the occasional finger. It felt wrong to have a group of adults make fun of us. The day before, when the other campers made a scene, it felt natural, cruel, but understandable, but to get the same treatment from the people who were supposed to be above us was just plain cruel.

Conversation between our little group was scarce while we ate: a couple of complaints about the food from Rodney, a line or two from Diego about his time being wasted, a random musing from Barry about how it was odd that tree roots didn't run into each other, and Dexter questioning out loud what we'd seen the night before. None of us bothered to answer him, instead choosing to keep our heads down and our focus elsewhere, until Director Downs threw one of the mess hall doors in.

"Mathews!" His eyes fixed on me, and I could see rage swirling behind his pupils. "To the docks, now!"

Be Grateful Or Else

Director Downs only demanded that I follow him to the docks, but my group came with me, Levi and Dexter included. He walked at a quick, angry pace, digging each step into the ground like he was mad at the dirt for being there. Not a word came from him or us until we reached the main dock and saw the carnage.

Two quick facts to keep in mind: first, Camp Alkali had three docks: one small dock by the boy's cabin and another by the girl's cabins, and a larger main dock situated between the two nearest to the mess hall. Second, the smaller docks were used for things like swimming and fishing, while the main dock was used for launching canoes, larger water sports, and the occasional diving activity. The main dock that Downs had led us to looked like it had been ran into by a speed boat.

"You care to explain how you pulled this one off, Eddie?" He asked with a clenched jaw.

"Lester, you think I did this?" I hoped using his first name would lighten the mood.

"Don't you 'Lester' me, boy!" It didn't. "I don't know how you did it or why, but you need to give me one good reason why I shouldn't report you to the authorities!"

Barry, being Barry, couldn't help himself but to ask the obvious. "Your name is Lester?"

Downs stomped his feet like a toddler and clenched his jaw so tight that I worried blood would start to trickle from his ears. He spoke through gritted teeth. "All of you, explain this. Now."

"Mr. Downs, sir," Levi stepped in front of me, acting as some kind of symbolic shield. "Do you have any kind of proof that these kids busted up the dock?"

"Proof?" Downs asked, sounding like a church pastor on the verge of a one-liner. "How's that for proof?"

He pointed to something floating in the water, towards the center of the lake, just far enough out that you had to squint and use your hand as a visor to see it. At first, I thought it was a log, probably blown into the lake by the storm we'd almost gotten caught in the night before. But the more I looked at it, the clearer the image became; it was the makeshift monster from the Anna Richards incident.

An old canoe retrofitted with stray 2x4s and scraps of plywood to look like the head of a sea creature. Painted a deep green that had faded some from the last time I saw it, with bright red eyes to really sell it. My friends and I cobbled it together in two late-night sessions that required us to sneak out of our cabin and fashion it with only hand tools. Before the prank had gone south, I was fairly proud of our little monster, but standing on the shore that day, it felt like a bad omen.

"What exactly am I looking at, sir?" Levi asked, staring intently.

Downs shot me a death glare. "Mind explaining to Mr. White what that is?"

I had an uncle who was a regular at the county drunk tank. He gave shit advice on almost everything, but he did teach me one thing that proved to be useful in life. "No, sir, I can't say I do." Plead the fifth.

"Edward Matthews, I will not hesitate to contact your parents!" He fumed.

"Alright, alright." The last thing I needed was a long car ride with Mom telling me every negative thing she'd ever thought about me. "It's a fake lake monster. We used it in a prank last year, and well, it didn't end well."

Levi's eyes went wide. "Anna Richards?"

I only nodded.

"Alright, so Eddie's dumb boat is on the water. What's that got to do with the docks?" Levi asked.

"You don't see it? Trouble-making kids are upset that they get stuck on maintenance duty, so they do what trouble-making kids do and pull a prank." He looked past Levi and right at us. "Very funny boys, the lake monster destroyed the docks. Ha. Ha. Ha."

"Now just hold on a second." Dexter stepped forward. "How in the world do you think we would have done that?" He gestures to the dock. "These are all cut up or pulled up. The boards are busted and splintered everywhere. It looks like a tree fell on it."

"Yeah, it was probably the storm." Barry added. "When we got caught in it last night, I thought we were gonna blow away. Right guys?"

All of us, Levi included, focused a hard stare on Bary while we telepathically debated if we should kill him then or later. A part of me hoped—and even prayed—that Downs hadn't caught what he said, but my prayer went unanswered. He let out a growl of frustration before drilling into us more.

"You were up past curfew? What in God's name were you doing? This?" He motioned to the dock. "Or some other terrible prank."

"Director Downs, believe me, sir, they weren't damaging anything; I found them in the woods." Levi raised his hands and motioned for him to calm down.

"In the woods?" He did not calm down. "How'd they end up in the woods, Mr. White? While under your care? Care to explain yourself?"

Levi swallowed hard and scrambled to find an answer. "Well, sir, you see, I, uh. You have to understand that, um, well." His eyes were darting between Downs and a woman watching us from down the shoreline.

My gut told me that was the gal he wanted to impress, and he was choking. "Lester, hear me out." I dared to interrupt. "The only reason we were able to sneak off to the woods was because you took Mr. White here to your office for a tongue-lashing about the skunk debacle. The only reason we decided to sneak off was to blow off some steam after being hosed down in front of every camper. So sir, if you're looking for someone to blame, I'd recommend looking in the mirror." Rodney let out an 'oh, damn!' and quickly covered his mouth. "And if all of that makes your blood boil, I'd like to remind you, before calling our parents, that we could and would inform them that we were attacked by animals, left unsupervised, and publicly humiliated all on your watch."

Downs face became so red that I would've bet he was on the verge of an aneurysm. "You wouldn't dare."

I shrugged and momentarily contemplated where that level of confidence had been all my life. "Maybe I would, maybe I wouldn't. Feel like rolling the dice, Lester?"

Downs took a deep breath, relaxed his shoulders, and rubbed his left temple. "Mr. White, it seems you and your crew have some repairs to complete. The dock needs to be usable by tomorrow, so I expect you all to work around the clock to get it done. Am I understood?"

Levi nodded, looking a bit relieved, and replied, "Yes, sir, I understand."

"Then hop to it." Downs left without giving us another look.

Once we were sure he was out of earshot, we all took an easy breath, and Diego broke into praise. "Holy shit Eddie, you played him like a fuckin' fiddle!"

"I thought we were screwed, and then you just swooped in and told him how it was. Oh my god!" Rodney added.

Levi looked down the shoreline at the mystery woman and started to jog towards her. He turned back and hollered, "I'll be right back. Don't break anything."

I was sure it was Olivia Burwell he was running to; the way he clammed up when he noticed her was the giveaway. All of us took a moment to watch as they interacted across the beach, and we took bets about what they were talking about. It was strange to watch; he was older than us and technically in charge of us, but when it came to having a crush, he acted much the same as we would. Walking the tightrope of being nervous and terrified and hoping to somehow land a foot at the appropriate level of confidence. They only chatted for a few minutes, then he was back, and we started our work.

The rest of that day was a slog of physical labor and an unforgiving sun. It took the whole morning to remove the damaged boards, most of the afternoon to retrieve the tools and materials we needed from the workshop that was tucked on a forgotten side of camp, and a fair chunk of the early evening to get the new planks installed. By the time it was all said and done, we were soaked in a combination of lake water and sweat and had a significantly higher chance of falling prey to skin cancer.

Lunch had been delivered to us by Mrs. Leaver, who asked how our day was going. When we told her we weren't enjoying it, she offered for us to come back and work with the kitchen crew again, which made us promptly stop complaining. Levi had given us a few snack cakes from a personal supply he kept hidden in the workshop at some point, and Olivia Burwell came just as the sun was setting to deliver us a brown bag meal for dinner. The sight of her heading toward us made Levi drop what he was doing and stand in attention.

"Evening Olivia." He said it, sounding parched.

"Evening yourself." She grinned. "You and your boys sure put in a hell of a day. It looks like you did good work."

"Thanks!" Diego said, sitting on the ground and waving a hammer. "It sucked, and we had no idea what we were doing."

"So if something breaks and you fall in, you can blame us." Dexter added as he finished nailing down a piece of railing.

"Ignore them." Levi waved a dismissive hand. "They held their own for the most part."

"Well, I just wanted to say thanks for fixing the dock and for dealing with that skunk problem under my cabin. My girls are feeling a lot better knowing they won't be attacked on their way to breakfast." She smiled wide while she spoke, so wide that her whole face seemed to beam.

"Is Megan alright?" Diego asked. He hadn't been able to meet up with her since the skunk incident happened, and he never got to gloat that he helped 'save' Megan's cabin. "Does she miss me?"

Olivia's beaming face shifted to a look of quiet disapproval. "You must be Deigo. Megan's new secret boyfriend."

"Boyfriend?" Diego blushed so hard that even after being under the beating sun all day, we could see him turn red. "She said I'm her boyfriend?"

"Did you hear her say secret? As in, probably ashamed of you." Rodney added.

"Rodney, don't make me come over there." Deigo pointed his hammer at him.

Olivia giggled, which made Rodney blush just as hard as Diego had. Getting a cute grown-up to laugh was the crown jewel of achievements for young guys like us.

"Well, I wanted to properly thank you all for your hard work." Olivia went back to beaming at us. "I already talked to Director Downs and got the OK for you guys to come to the beach fire tonight. Give you a chance to relax a bit and hang out with kids your age."

After the scene I made that morning, I couldn't believe that Downs would reward us. "He said that? Lester? After the whole deal about us supposedly breaking the dock in the first place?"

"Well, he did say something about telling you boys to remember this kindness." She shrugged, looking a tad uncomfortable.

"There it is." Dexter said, finishing his work and taking a seat on the ground. "Be grateful or else. What a joke."

"Count us in." Levi decided for us. "We'll show up around sundown if that works."

"Perfect." She gave us all a cute wave and started walking away.

"Look at that ass." Barry murmured with his head cocked.

Levi tossed a water bottle at him. "Shut up."

It took the rest of the evening to get the tools and wood scraps back to the workshop and get cleaned up. The only options for showers at Camp Alkali were the ones by the beach set up for rinsing sand off kids or the locker rooms attached to the north side of the gymnasium. There was a locker room for boys and girls equipped with eight lockers and eight shower stalls that only had a hazed plastic film to use as a door. Showering at camp was not for the faint of heart or the shy.

We'd all been to camp before and knew the routine, so we silently went about our business of shedding our disgusting clothes, stuffing them in a laundry bag, setting out new ones, wrapping ourselves in a towel that was likely originally purchased in the 80s, and getting showered. A few jokes were cracked, but for the most part, we kept to ourselves, except for Barry. He took the stall right next to me, and for the first time since camp started, he seemed to have his head on straight.

"Eddie?"

"What's up?"

"You got any idea what busted up the docks like that?"

I did, but I knew that saying a lake monster did it would be met with ridicule, so I played dumb. "The storm, I guess. Those winds last night were insane."

"But what about those green lights?" He paused for a moment. "That feeling is in the air. You felt that too, didn't you?"

I couldn't think of a good lie, so I spoke low. "Yeah. Something felt off. But none of that matters. It's not like Downs is going to believe anything we tell him." I turned the water off and reached for the towel hanging next to the sheet of plastic that separated me from the larger room.

Barry did the same and asked a question I was surprised I hadn't asked. "Yeah, I guess so, but you know what I can't stop thinking about? How'd that old prank boat get out there? Wouldn't they have gotten rid of it after last year?"

The question made my hair stand on end; he was right. Maybe I was being framed; there was no lake monster smashing up the camp. I was being targeted. But by whom and why? It didn't make any sense.

I wrapped the towel around myself and stepped out of the shower. Sitting on one of the locker room benches was Dexter, staring at the ground. His face was twisted in a way I'd learned to look out for. A look that screamed, 'Don't look at me, I didn't do it', a look I'd memorized over the years.

He looked up at me. "The fuck are you looking at?"

The Classic Story

There didn't seem to be much point in confronting Dexter in the locker room. Either he had something to do with the old monster boat showing up, or he didn't. I didn't have evidence that pointed in either direction and knew he'd deny anything I tried to pin on him, so I kept my mouth shut.

Once we were showered and had mostly removed the smell of lake muck from our bodies, we got dressed and headed to the shore to meet up with the other campers. I should have been excited, or at least a bit curious, but I was dreading it. While Diego planned to sneak off with Megan and Rodney and Barry discussed their wingman strategies, I kept kicking a question around in my head. What actually ripped apart the docks? And why did I have a feeling I didn't want to know the answer?

The walk from the gymnasium to the beach party wasn't fair, and before long we could see beach fires and hear music playing on underwhelming speakers. When we strode into the firelight, Olivia was there to greet us and introduce us to her five campers. Beth Schaffer, Kaya Smit, Missy O'Connor, Camila Jefferson, and the already-infamous Manic Megan Drakos. Each of them thanked us for dealing with their skunk problem and apologized on behalf of the camp for the ridicule we faced afterward. Admittedly, an apology like that would usually be cold comfort, but coming from a cabin of girls made my teenage heart much more open to it.

"You," Megan grabbed Diego by his collar and began to pull him away. "Are mine, tiger."

"Remember what we said about making good choices!" Olivia called as the pair of them walked away toward a different fire.

"She's so, like, pushy. It's gross." Missy O'Connor said this through her wire braces. She was a pale-skinned girl with brown hair pulled into a ponytail. "What does he see in her?"

"Digeo?" Rodney pondered the question seriously for a moment. "Honestly, I think he just wants to feel seen, you know?"

"Oh, wow, yeah, that makes sense," Missy replied, before letting her hair down. "You want to go chill by the fire?"

"Yeah, maybe we could introduce you guys to some of the others." Camila added, Give Barry a once-over.

"By all means, lead the way." Rodney gave them a half-bow and started walking with them toward the crowd.

"Righteous," Barry said, before slapping me on the back. "You coming, Eddie?"

"I'm alright. Catch you later." I didn't have it in me to pretend that I knew how to flirt.

Olivia and Levi slipped away to a bench by one of the fires, and Dexter had disappeared to god knows where. That left Kaya and myself standing aimlessly in the humid night air as the chattering sound of socializing buzzed around us. When Olivia had invited us to a beach party, I expected a small fire and maybe some marshmallows, but that night was buzzing with the palpable energy of poor choices about to happen.

"You want to go somewhere quieter?" Kaya asked.

Maybe she could see this discomfort on my face, or maybe she hated being there as much as I did. "You got something in mind?"

She motioned for me to follow her, and my shy legs propelled me forward.

The beach itself must have looked like a swarm of ants from a birds-eye view. Campers and counselors mingled around four different bonfires while some music played on outdated boomboxes and rolled out of the occasional acoustic guitar. Most of the kids were just chatting, laughing, and swapping stories, while others made themselves comfortable by roasting hotdogs and constructing smores, and of course, the bravest among them dared to retreat beyond the firelight with lustful intent. Summer camp rarely gets a reputation for debauchery, but make no mistake, the whole concept dances around the responsibility of keeping horny teenagers off each other.

Kaya led me to a bench on the dock I'd just finished working on earlier that day. "Thanks for fixing the dock too. They're really keeping you guys busy, huh?"

I scoffed and took a seat next to her. "Gotta pay penance for our actions. Or something like that, at least."

"What happened?"

"One of the guys in my cabin punched me in the face, and well, we were already on thin ice from something that happened last year."

She looked at me with curiously peering eyes. Kaya had tanned skin, green eyes that glimmered in the moonlight, and dirty blonde hair chopped in a bob. I'd never seen a girl who looked like her. After a few moments, her curious look evaporated and was replaced with a look of realization.

"You guys caused the whole lake monster incident, right?" Her voice had a layer of disdain in it.

I felt myself plush; even under my sunburned cheeks, I could tell my whole face had gone red. "It's not something I'm proud of, and if Dexter hadn't gotten in the way, it wouldn't have been such a disaster."

"Dexter? Let me guess, he's the one who tried to break your nose."

I looked away from her and fixed my eyes on the highlighted waves coming to shore. "How'd you know?"

"The way you said his name." She followed my gaze to the wave. "You said it like you wanted to kill him."

I let out a laugh, perhaps too comfortably. "Kill is a strong word. Would I maybe count to ten before throwing him a lifeline? Maybe, depending on my mood."

"Well, for what it's worth, Anna turned out alright. All things considered." She looked away from the waves and back to the flickering bonfires on the shore.

I felt my stomach do a flip. "You know Anna Richards?"

"Well, yeah, remember?" She looked at me with anticipation, like I was supposed to deliver the punch line of a joke. After a moment of silence, she said, "Oh my god, you don't remember me."

"I'm sorry." My brain started doing flips, looking for a memory of her or a good excuse. "I'm shit with faces and not much better with names."

She waved a hand dismissively. "It's fine. I'm her cousin, and I was in her cabin.

"Oh, so you were..."

Kaya cut me off. "When she almost died because of a prank gone sideways? Yeah, I was there. I didn't just hear about the rumors."

"I'm sorry." The words came out like a reflex, unsure of what I was actually apologizing for. "That whole thing was a bad idea."

"Well, if she'd remembered her inhaler, it might have been funny." She let out a nervous laugh. "You should have heard her scream. She believed in that story more than anyone else. Swear to God."

"Really?" I let out a few nervous laughs of my own.

"Oh, for sure. Anna memorized that campfire story word for word." She started to snicker.

"To be fair, it's a good story." Our laughter started to die out.

In the distance, we heard an eruption of laughter, and I looked over and could see Barry standing by one of the fires, moving erratically. He'd found himself at the center of attention, like he usually did, and was probably telling some big fish story, trying to get a rise out of everyone he could. Barry was a force of nature, no doubting that.

"So why'd you come back this year? You know, if you were just going to get in trouble for the whole Anna situation," Kaya asked as she got up from the bench and walked farther out on the dock.

"I didn't have much of a choice." I followed her to the edge of the dock, where we both slipped our shoes off and dipped our feet into the water. "My mom is dead set on seeing me as little as possible, so I go to a lot of camps. How about you?

I'm sure your family wasn't thrilled about your cousin almost drowning here."

"I didn't really give them a choice." She looked over her shoulder and stared at Barry in the distance, still making a fool of himself. "I love it here. They knew if they kept me at home, I'd just raise hell."

A cacophony of applause rose from the beach, and Kaya and I knew a camp tradition was taking place. "Should we go? Be a shame to miss the annual story."

Kaya shrugged. "Might as well."

We walked back barefoot, with our shoes in hand, and arrived at the bonfire just in time. Every year at Camp Alkali, they have a beach fire and tell the tale of the Alkali Lake Monster. Some years it's a full production with sound CDs and shadow puppets, and another year it's a more intimate telling. That year, Director Downs kept it simple. He'd stood up on a log next to the largest of the four bonfires and began to tell the tale while his face bathed in the firelight.

"Most of you have already heard the stories." Downs voice bellowed, and everyone fell silent. "Some of you have even seen flashes of the things moving like a serpent in the water, gliding on its way without bothering to notice you. But tonight, while the tide crashes behind us, I'm going to tell you a new story."

A small chorus of cheers broke out, and Kaya and I shared a glance that said, 'Oh boy, here we go' before we looked back at Downs.

He told the classic story about a lake monster that supposedly started as a salamander, mutated by radioactive waste, and went on to eat livestock, terrifying passersby. But that night, he took the story in a different direction, a more personal direction, and told a story we didn't expect he'd ever share. Lester Downs stood upon his log and told us about his time as a camper and his own run-in with the monster.

According to the story, when Lester was about our age, he came to Camp Alkali for the first time and fell in love with all parts of it. He was eager to get out on the water. As a boy who lived with corn fields on all sides of him, the idea of navigating any body of water made him feel alive. On the third day of camp, he finally got his shot and took his first kayaking lesson with the other boys from his cabin. Downs claimed he took to it like a duck to water and got cocky enough to split from his group into the open water.

His councilor hollered at him to rejoin the group, but he ignored him, something he urged us to never do, and kept paddling into the expanse of the lake. After some time passed, he could no longer hear the frustrated calls of his councilor, and the shore was almost out of sight. He found himself alone with just water on all sides, except he didn't feel alone. That feeling that someone was watching you, but not just watching you, watching you with intent, washed over him. It was silly to think anyone would even pay attention to him all the way out there on the lake, but still, the feeling was hard to ignore.

Downs said that he glared across the horizon, looking for another kayak or even a figure on the blurry shore, but found nothing. His gut told him that it was time to get off the water and head back, but he realized he'd gone so far out that he'd lost track of where he'd come from. He began to panic a little and tried to pick a direction to start paddling when he felt something bump against his boat. Something solid, with force, not soft or passive like a piece of driftwood.

He dared to look into the depths below him and saw something circling the kayak, and he caught a glimpse of two deep green orbs that seemed to peer up at him. His heart about burst from his chest at the sight of it, and he began paddling frantically in an attempt to escape from whatever it was. The thing followed him, lurking just below the water, until he saw a chunk of land just ahead of him.

Downs said his hands damn near bled from how quickly he sliced his paddle through the water as he put all he had into making it to land. Just as he saw the shallows start to come into view, he felt something rise from the water behind him, spraying him as it rose. He didn't dare to look; he just kept paddling and paddling until he was beached.

He took in huge gasps of air as he scrambled from his kayak to the rocky shore, and he realized a shadow was cast over him. Down dared to look behind him and saw a towering, slimy, bull-headed thing staring at him from the water. A scream escaped his lips as he got to his feet and ran inland. But the thing didn't follow; still, for good measure, he said he climbed a tree and waited.

The chunk of land he found himself on was an island, deep in the lake, and far from the view of camp. He knew he'd have to make his way back, but he couldn't bring himself to get on the water again. At least not that night. Downs said he spent the night in a small forest, with a fire just big enough to ward off any creepy crawlies. When first light hit, he paddled to the next closest shore, hiked back to camp, and was met with stern talking, of course. No one believed him when he told them what had happened, and he didn't blame them. He barely believed it had happened.

The crowd had grown dead still, and the three other fires had been abandoned and left to smolder. Not a soul dared to interrupt him as he wrapped up, sprinkling in more details for good measure. He had everyone eating out of the palm of his hand, and you could tell we were buying every word of it. Even I was transfixed until I felt Kaya tugging at my shirt.

"What?" I whispered.

"Do you see that?" She nodded to the lake. "Just beyond the dock."

I turned to look and felt the hairs on my neck stand on end, because what Kaya pointed out wasn't strange to me anymore. A dim green glow seemed to glide just below the surface of the water, moving towards the shore. Initially, I stood up, trying to make sense of what I was seeing and fighting for an explanation. As I stood there, I could feel eyeballs on me as the rest of the campers looked at me, wondering what I was doing.

"Eddie, what in God's name are you doing?" Downs asked, dropping his story-telling voice.

My hand shook as I raised it, pointing to the water. "Ya'll see that too, right?"

Everyone stood up to look at the water, and in one swift motion, a bulky black figure erupted from under the water. People screamed, people cursed, and some people even started running from the beach. I just stood there, frozen in fear and disbelief, while I told myself it couldn't be real; there was no way in hell a lake monster was real. My leg still refused to move when the figure rose higher and inches closer and then removed its head.

Lester Downs broke out in laughter. "Oh lord! Eddie, you should have seen your face!"

I'm So Fired

The whole thing was a prank that Lester went to work on as soon as he left us to repair the docks. It was the only reason he allowed Olivia to invite us to the beach party in the first place—a chance at payback for damaging his dock (which we didn't do). To his credit, it worked; I looked like the biggest goddamn moron in the state that night. And he made sure I knew it.

He'd cobbled together a monster costume out of an old wetsuit, some snorkeling gear, a bike helmet, and two oversized glow sticks. In the daylight, it would have looked like the kind of outfit a doomsday prophesier would wear, but in the dark water, it worked perfectly. I found out years later that Downs had to pay a kitchen worker $50 to agree to play the part of the monster because he was paranoid that if he asked a counselor to do it, they might spill the beans.

To his credit, he didn't call me out by name too much, just enough for me to know that the whole thing was personal. After the commotion had died down and the staff called it a night, Downs informed Levi that his crew of misfits would be in charge of clean-up since we were the makeshift maintenance crew for a few more days. So while the others got to head back to their cabin for some well-earned rest, we were cleaning up trash by moonlight and making sure the campfires were fully extinguished.

Sleep came easy that night, half because we were exhausted from the work and half because we were likely sleep-deprived. The next morning had an odd sense of rhythm to it. Levi woke us up, we got dressed, went to breakfast, and ate amongst ourselves. We followed Levi to the camp's main road, where he had us help with some landscaping, and then we grabbed our sack lunches and headed back to The Hole. No one skipped out that afternoon to go do their own thing; we all stuck together eating lunch on our bunks, even Dexter.

"All I'm saying is that this hardly counts as a sandwich." Dexter held up two crusty pieces of bread with a thin spread of PB&J on them.

He was right. The sack lunches we'd gotten from day one weren't anything to write home about, but that day they felt suspiciously shitty. "You think they're out to get us or something?" I asked.

"For what?" Barry chimed in, his mouth half full of that day's mystery baked good. "We didn't do anything to the kitchen crew."

"Maybe they just hate us." I replied before biting into my own sad excuse of a sandwich.

Levi got up from his bunk and forced open one of the cabin's windows. "I wouldn't put it past them." He added. "Most of the guys down there have a weird sense of humor."

"You been hanging around those guys a lot, Mr. White?" Rodney asked while eying his food suspiciously.

Levi made a face and walked back to his bunk. "Gotta remember, I've been here since the start of the season, and you boys just got here. Let's just say they ain't my crowd."

Diego poked his head up from the top bunk he'd claimed on the first day. "Aw, come on, Levi, tell us what's wrong with them. Are they felons? Drug dealers? Inbred?"

"What?" Levi shouted. "No. What is wrong with you, Diego? It's nothing like that. After the first camp ended, they invited me out on the staff boat with them, and they thought it'd be funny to leave me in the lake. Just a cruel prank to pull, that's all."

None of us spoke for a minute while we processed the fact that Levi was just an older version of us, a misfit who paid taxes. Then something dawned on Dexter. "Did you say a staff boat?"

"Yeah, what of it?"

"Is it a big boat? Like a real boat, with an engine and stuff?" Dexter's voice rose a tad, giving away his excitement.

"Why are you askin'?" Levi gave him a hard stare.

Dexter sat all the way up. "Well, what if we used the boat to go have some fun? Beats hanging out in the cabin or sulking in the woods. Right guys?" He looked around the room for support.

"It could be cool to go fishing." Barry added.

"Or to take the girls out on." Diego replied, his eyes wide with daydreams.

"Now hold on." Levi stood up and placed his hands on his hips. "We are not stealing camp property because you guys are bored. If you're bored, I can find more jobs for you to do."

"If you do that, then you'll have to do the jobs with us." I reminded him. "Maybe you could just show up the boat, and then we can find some middle ground. What do you think?"

"All in favor?" Dexter asked.

Everyone said 'aye," except for Levi. He hung his head and spoke in a defeated tone, "Fine. Fuck me, fine. Follow me."

We followed him out of the cabin and headed away from the main campus into the woods. He told us to keep our voices down and that if we ran into anyone, we were supposed to tell them we were on our way to organize the shack, whatever that meant. The path we followed was thin, barely used, and slowly descended closer and closer to the water until we reached our destination. A covered dock in the shade of the pine forest, far enough away from the shores of camp for anyone to see.

Once it came into view, we could all see the boat—a proper speed boat—just sitting there, begging to be taken out on the water.

"Now that's a boat." Dexter said, jogging toward it.

"Don't touch anything." Levi barked.

Dexter threw his hand up. "Alright, alright. Don't need to get testy about it."

"Well, well, well, look what I found." Rodney kicked a bucket with a few fishing rods placed inside. "What do you say, Mr. White, care for a bit of fishing on the boat? Sure beats planting more flowers, don't you think?"

"No. Not happening." Levi stood his ground. "If Downs catches you guys on this boat, I'm done for. Let's go."

Just then, the noise of an engine startled us all, except for Barry who was standing behind the wheel. "It looks like someone left the keys in it."

"Fuck yes! Let's go!" Diego yelled as he hopped onboard.

We all followed as Levi protested from the dock. "Turn it off right now, Barry! I'm not fucking joking."

"Don't be such a stick in the mud!" Dexter yelled. "Fucking grow a pair and let's go."

Levi looked up the path we'd traveled nervously, then back at us. Barry had already started to pull the boat out of the dock and didn't seem to plan on stopping. We watched as Levi took a few steps back and then ran and jumped off the dock, barely landing in the boat with a thud.

Rodney picked him up and slapped him on the shoulder. "Way to live a little, Mr. White."

"I'm so fired." Levi said while catching his breath.

To our surprise, Barry actually knew how to pilot the boat. It turned out that his dad was an avid fisherman, and Barry often got put in charge of lugging his dad around his favorite fishing spots on Sundays. There was some arguing about what we should do or where we should go, but we knew that no plan was a poor plan. We agreed that we'd head back to the dock right after making one stop.

"The stories all say they had a shack or hut. So if we see a shack, then we know we should come back and look." Dexter said as Barry pulled the boat up on the island.

Up close, it was bigger than I'd pictured, but it was still quite small. I asked, "You sure this is the same one you showed us from the hill?"

"It's the only island in the lake." Levi added. "No one ever goes here, though."

"Barry, just go around the whole thing." Dexter ordered. "I just want to give it a once-over."

"Yes, sir, captain, sir." Barry answered in a terrible pirate voice.

The boat circled the island as slowly as Barry could go, and all of us, Levi included, had our eyes glued to it. For being such a small patch of land, it was densely packed with tall pine trees, and a few signs of humanity scattered the shore. Trash mostly, an overturned faded orange canoe, and a car tire stuck out the most. Just as we were rounding the last section of the island, something shiny caught my eye.

"There!" I pointed toward it. I could barely make out a small structure with what looked like a tin roof. "A metal roof, back in the trees. You guys see that.

"Well, I'll be damned." Levi whispered.

"Fuckin' knew it!" Dexter fist pumped in the air.

Diego squinted as he stared. "Looks like we got ourselves a loveshack, boys."

We all stared at him in contempt, but Barry said what we were all thinking. "Gross, Diego. That's just gross."

Levi demanded that we go back to the dock and get to work on our next project (painting all the signage in camp) before Downs realized we were gone. None of us tried to stop him, mostly because Dexter agreed with Levi and said he needed to gather supplies before we headed back out. The two of them had some back and forth about whether we'd ever go back, but their argument was cut short. As we approached the dock, we saw Downs standing with his arms crossed.

"Alright." Levi swallowed hard. "Follow my lead."

Barry parked the boat right where he'd found it, and before any of us could step off to tie the boat down, Downs started barking. "Mr. White, what in the blazes are you doing?"

"What am I doing?" Levi matched his energy. "I'm doing my job, sir. Do you have any idea how much trash has built up on the island? Mounds, sir, mounds!"

Downs looked at him, stunned. "What are you talking about?"

"We were cleaning up some of the hiking paths this afternoon and ran into a Park Ranger. He said there were reports of campfires on the island and asked if it was our campers."

"Well, of course it wasn't." Downs stuttered his words a bit.

"That's what I thought, but I figured I'd go check." Levi motioned to the boat. "I took the boys with me for good measure, and you know what we found?"

Downs' eyes jumped to each of our faces nervously. "Trash?"

"Yes, trash—lots of it. It seems your councilors haven't been running a very tight shit, sir, pardon the pun, and campers have been sneaking off." Levi walked past him, and he tied the boat to the dock. "Tomorrow we'll be heading out there to do some cleanup. But I suggest you have a meeting about this."

"Right." Downs gave us a nod. "As you were then, Sorry to intrude, Mr. White." He turned in a quick one step motion and began trekking back up the path to camp.

Once Downs was out of earshot, Dexter looked to Levi with wide eyes. "I thought you didn't want to go back there."

Levi shrugged. "I've been curious about the place since I was a camper. This way, we have an excuse to go out there without sneaking off."

Rodney slapped him on the back. "Clever like a fox, Mr. White."

We went about the rest of our day as planned, helping Levi paint signs around camp and heading to the mess hall for dinner. We decided to eat with the campers that night, feeling that we'd mostly moved on from our public hosedown, and it felt good to hear the sounds of people around us as we ate. Levi went off to eat with some other staff, and Diego found Manic Megan, who insisted on sitting with us.

"So you guys get to go check out the haunted island?" She almost squealed.

"Isn't it awesome, babe?" Diego had his arm around her as he tried to stare down at her shirt.

"You really think it's haunted by some outlaw ghosts?" I asked. "Don't you think that's a little on the nose?"

"Outlaw ghosts?" Megan looked at me, confused. "Like cowboys and shit?"

"Well yeah," Dexter leaned in, like he was about to reveal covert intelligence. "The James Riley Gang. You heard the stories, right?"

Megan shook her head and took a bite of her food. "I don't know anything about no cowboy ghost."

"Then why do you think the island is haunted?" Rodney asked.

Megan took a moment to swallow her food. "Because of those two kids who died out there last year."

Windfall

Life in the pre-internet age seems unthinkable by modern standards. Mostly because you couldn't do a web search to verify a story, you just had to take people's word on it, and that's what we did with Megan. She told us that after the camp season ended last year, there were reports of some kids, in their early twenties, who robbed a string of truck stops and gas stations along Highway 2. According to her, there were newspaper articles that said the boys came to Lake Alkali after being chased down by the State Patrol, but they lost them in the woods. They eventually used a helicopter to look for them, but didn't see any sign of them. It was like they vanished.

"That's a load of bullshit." Rodney leaned back in his chair and crossed his arms. "You're pulling our chain, ain't you?"

"Why would I have any reason to lie?" She matched his body language.

Diego came to her defense. "Yeah, Rodney, why?"

"Think about it. We saw that canoe out there. Maybe it was theirs." Dexter sounded sincerely interested. "Right, Megan?"

"Could be," Megan said, uncrossing her arms and leaning toward the table. "Apparently, they were never found. Just, poof, gone. I even heard a couple of kids here say that their stash is still on that island."

Before we could debate any further, Downs rang the dinner bell, signaling to everyone that mealtime was over.

"Let me know what you guys find out there." Megan said as she got up from the table and walked away.

"There's no harm in looking for hidden treasure, right?" Barry asked.

"Now you believe her too?" Rodney looked at him, seeming a bit hurt. "It's a ghost story."

"Yeah, well, this whole place is just a bunch of ghost stories. Some of 'em got to be real." Barry insisted, and I agreed with him.

"He's right." Dexter added.

"No one asked you, trailer trash. Eddie, talk some sense into them. Please, man." Rodney looked at me for backup.

I let out a deep sigh as I searched for the right words. "I don't buy it. But if we stumble upon a box full of old bills, I won't complain."

Rodney threw up his hands in defeat. "Fine. I guess we'll go treasure hunting."

That night in The Hole, we all pestered Levi about exactly how much work we were expected to do the next day and how much free time we could anticipate. He was tight-lipped, though, telling us to let him worry about the details but still be ready to do some heavy lifting. We groaned and bickered some, but he reminded us that if we didn't want to be helpful on the island, we were welcome to stay back and clean toilets. Sleep came easy after that threat.

The next morning, he'd woken us up much earlier than we'd woken up the other days. We woke up so early that breakfast wasn't even ready yet, so Levi had made a thermos of coffee and snagged some packaged honey buns from the mess hall for our morning meal. After slowly slugging through our food, he marched us out the door, into the woods, and down to the covered dock.

He'd loaded the boat with all kinds of supplies that we could find—trash bags, rakes, shovels, a gas can, solar panels, a power converter, and other things I swore we didn't need. It was packed so tight that there was barely enough room for us all to fit in. Levi insisted that we trust his instincts and try not to move around too much, which let us know even he knew he'd gone overboard on the supplies.

The sun had just begun to rise when we got to shore and started to unload everything. In the stillness of the morning, the island had a much more ominous feeling to it. The darkness of pre-dawn made the speck of forest look like it went on forever, daring someone to wander into its depths. I started at it for a bit too long and felt a shudder run down my spine, which Dexter must have noticed.

"What's the matter, Eddie? Scared of the woods." Dexter went to punch me on the shoulder, but I swatted his hand out of the way.

"Try it again, and I'll drown you." The words came out of me like a reflex; I didn't even mean to say it.

"Is that a threat?" Dexter flashed a wicked grin. One that I'd seen plenty of in previous years, but barely that year.

In a way, I suppose it was, but more than anything, I just wanted him to stop existing, which was a bit much to ask. So instead of letting him into my skin, I figured I'd get under his. "Why'd you keep the monster's head?"

That wicked grin unfurled into a look of surprise. "Monster head? What do you mean?"

"The prank with Anna Richards—that monster head. The one I built and used to scare the shit out of everyone. Someone kept it around, and then it showed up yesterday when the docks were busted up. Where'd you stash it?" I stepped closer to him and dug my finger into his chest. "You tryin' to get me banned for life or something? What are you up to?"

Barry had been watching us from a bit further inland and called out, "Just kiss already."

Everyone laughed, even Levi.

Dexter pulled my finger off of him. "Fuck you, Matthews." He stomped off toward the boat to grab the last of the supplies.

Levi put us to work cleaning up the rocky shoreline first, having us work all the way around the island. Everything you could think of had washed up there. Bottles, bags, articles of clothing, cigarette packs, and disposable cups—just to name a few things—and we filled almost half a dozen fifty-five-gallon bags with just trash. Once he was happy with that, around ten that morning, we made our way inland and immediately saw a small building.

It sat square in the center of the island, about eight feet wide and six feet long, with red-painted wood siding and a tin roof. By all accounts, it was more of a shed than a building, but it still seemed out of place. It had no windows and looked like it had only a swing door that was bolted shut. All of us stood and stared at it for a bit, everyone seemingly afraid to move any closer.

"So, there's definitely a dead body in there." Diego dared to speak first.

"What the hell are you talking about?" Levi asked.

"Megan said that two guys hid out here after robbing a few joints. So my guess is, one of the dudes locked the other one in there so he didn't have to split cash and then ran off."

"Do you think it's a skeleton by now?" Barry asked while scratching at his face.

"Nah," Diego said while walking closer to the building. "It takes longer than a year for a body to completely rot. Right Dexter?"

Dexter was taken aback by the question. "How would I know that?"

Diego shrugged before picking up a large rock off the ground. "You just seem like the type of dude that would know."

Weirdly enough, I agreed.

Diego raised the rock above his head and then smashed it down against the lock.

It didn't break on the first hit; it took three, but when it finally did give out, there was a hesitation from all of us about opening it. Rodney told Diego to, and Diego said Rodney should, but in the end, Levi stepped forward and pulled the door open. I'd like to say we were subtle and slowly approached the door, but the truth was that once it was open, we nearly knocked each other over to get a look inside.

I was as plain as a shed could be—stud walls, plywood floor, a small stack of firewood in one corner, a few hand tools in the other—but there was one thing out of place—a small cashbox sitting in the center of it all. It was green-painted metal with a thick coat of dust on it. By the look of it, I would have guessed it wasn't that old, which made me think that maybe Megan's story had some truth to it.

"I'll be damned." Levi muttered.

"How much do you think is in the box?" Diego asked, stepping into the building.

"One way to find out." Dexter pushed past all of us and kneeled down next to the cashbox.

There was no lock on it, but some rust had formed on the hinge, so it took a good tug from Dexter before the lid gave way. Once he had it open, we all poured in around him to see what was inside the cashbox. It wasn't the gold coins of some outlaw gang, but crumpled-together bills and rolls of coins. It's exactly the kind of loot you'd expect from a string of gas station robberies. The only logical thing to do was to count it all.

All in all, the cashbox held a bit more than six thousand dollars in assorted bills and coins.

"Holy fucking Christ, that's a lot of money." Barry said, sounding the most down-to-earth I'd ever heard him. "Like, wow, a lot of money."

"We gotta call this into the Rangers." Levi said it with panic in his eyes. "This is stolen money. No good can come from this."

All of us flinched at the same time and uttered a sound that almost resembled the words stop, no, or don't.

"Mr. White, you're a smart man. Let's just talk this over for a minute." Rodney went to put his hand on Levi's shoulder.

Levi grabbed his hand and tossed it away. "No. I said no, and that's final. I'm not letting you kids talk me into any more trouble."

"Just take a second to think about it." Dexter pleaded. "There's enough here for us to split it six ways. We'll each walk out of here with a grand."

That made Levi pause, and I watched as he mulled it over in his mind. In the couple of days I'd known him Levi White had already proven to be a morally gray individual. Seemingly striving to do what he thought was just or right, he was also willing to bend his ethics if you dangled the right carrot in front of his face. Sitting there in that misplaced shack, I knew that he was homeless and broke, so the promise of a sizeable windfall would be hard for him to ignore.

After a moment of internal debate, he said, "If word ever got out, we'd be in huge trouble. You understand that, don't you, Dexter?"

"It's worth the risk." Dexter said it without missing a beat. "I could use it." He shifted uncomfortably.

Diego, Barry, and Rodney all weighed in with their own reasons why we should keep the money, ranging from starting a college fund to buying a paintball gun, but the nervous look didn't leave Levi's eyes.

"Sorry boys. It ain't worth the jail time." He stood his ground.

I thought about what I'd do with the money. There were the usual ideas about new clothes, video games, or trying to impress a girl, but I couldn't figure out how to actually spend the money. A mother as overbearing as mine would catch on fast to a sudden influx of cash in my pocket and demand answers or take it for herself. Actually, knowing her, it'd probably be both. Besides, my home life was shit, but I was doing okay with material possessions.

"You can have my share." The words came out more assertive than I intended them to be.

"You mean it?" Levi looked puzzled.

"I won't get away with smuggling that much cash at home, there is no way in hell, so you can have it. If you keep your mouth shut and help us get it out of here, deal?" I stuck my hand out to shake it.

He chewed on the idea for a minute, mulling over his options, trying to decide which side of the line he'd stand on that day. Finally, he shook my hand. "Deal."

Crocodile Or Alligator?

As was standard practice for us that summer, we had a plan, but it wasn't a good one. We divided the cash up the way we had agreed on—two grand for Levi and one grand for the others—and stashed each share back in the cashbox. There was debate about where to hide the money while we waited for camp to end, but Levi convinced everyone that it was the safest place, for it was right where we'd found it, and said that he'd have us come out for another fake maintenance job to collect it. Everyone made peace with that plan, except for Dexter, who wanted to take an extra step.

"For all we know, Downs might want to come out here and inspect our work. We need to hide the box." Dexter was acting like his very existence depended on what we did with the money.

"Even if he could get off his ass long enough to do that, where would we hide it? It's a small shed." Rodney was standing in front of the door while he spoke, trying to show he was in control of the situation. "Besides, for all we know, you're up to something. Maybe you're thinking about hiding the loot and swiping it for yourself."

"Seriously?" Dexter stepped toward him and craned his head upward to match Rodney's stare. "You guys trust me that little? Name one time I stabbed you in the back."

Rodney furrowed his brow. "You put glue on my Kyayk seat two years ago, remember? My trunks got stuck to the boat, and I had to run back to the cabin with my hands covering my junk."

"You and a few of your buddies held me down my first year here and stuck gum in my hair. A whole pack. Nurse Linda had to shave my head." Diego pointed to the top of his skull. "It took a whole year to grow it back!"

"You put shrimp in my pillow case last year." Barry added.

"So?" Dexter's face was beginning to look panicked. "That's pretty harmless, Barry. Sorry, your pillow got wet." He scoffed.

"Mother fucker, I'm allergic to shellfish!" Barry stepped forward and shoved Dexter against the wall.

Barry had Dexter pinned; Diego and Rodney were crowded around him. "Let's all just calm down now." Dexter's voice lost its annoyed tone and was replaced with one that danced between spooked and surprised. "Eddie, tell these guys I'm not that bad. We're friends now, right?"

I had leverage. "Tell me the truth."

"What?" His tone landed on terrified.

"You said you didn't know anything about the fake monster I made or how it ended up on the lake yesterday. Tell me the truth. You know something, don't you?"

Dexter tried to thrash against Barry, but it was no use; Diego and Rodney pinned his arms down. "I don't know anything, swear on God."

"We could just leave him here, couldn't we, Rodney?" The words felt cold as they left me.

Rodney pushed on him harder. "Fine by me, Eddie. Fine by me."

"I hid it in the tree line." Dexter practically screamed the words. "After the whole thing was over, I could see how upset you were, so I hid it." Barry let him go, and he took a deep breath. "I just knew that if I could work it into a prank, it'd knock the wind out of you, hopefully for good. You know what I mean? Just really take you down a peg. But I didn't drag it out yesterday. The storm must have blown it into the tide or something like that."

I wanted to punch him; hell, I even balled up my fist to do just that, but Levi could sense the escalation. "Are ya'll done measuring dicks yet?" The question threw us for a loop. No one answered. "Good, that was painful to watch. Now, I agree with Dexter that if someone came looking, leaving the money out would be a bad idea, but I also trust Dexter about as much as I'd trust a coyote with a baby. Eddie's the only one not taking a cut, so he gets to choose the hiding spot."

Diego, Rodney, and Barry agreed it made sense; Dexter didn't dare to speak.

Levi had the others start loading trash bags and supplies back into the boat, and he told me to go burry the money somewhere in the trees. I wrapped the cashbox in a plastic bag in a half-hearted attempt to keep moisture out and walked into the grove of towering pines while I tried to listen to the muffled sound of the others on the beach, but I couldn't make out anything definitive. My eyes were drawn to a tree that was cracked from the top to about half way down, with dead yellow branches (stuck by lighting, my guess), and I figured it was a memorable enough tree to use as a marker.

I'd brought a small hand shovel with me from the shed and dug a hole just big enough to cover the cash box. It was a snug fit, but I made it work and covered it with dirt, and I wondered if pirates really buried their treasure like all the stories said. Once I was happy with the job I'd done, I stood up and began looking for a rock or something to mark the spot, just in case the tree wasn't enough.

"Eddie, are you almost done in there?" Levi bellowed from the shore.

"Almost. Give me another minute." As I hollered back I felt something snap under my foot.

I looked down to see what it was, thinking it must have been a twig or something like that, and saw white dust starting to rise. My mind raced trying to think of what could be under my shoe, but I came up with no answer, so I lifted it up and saw a jawbone cracked in half. At first I thought it must have been from a deer or something, but then it seemed too square, and I remembered I was on a speck of an island, and then I took a closer look at the teeth. Human teeth.

"Guys...." I began to call out before a firm feeling washed over me.

It was dizziness, not disorientation, like the way I felt when Dexter cold-cocked me that first day. I couldn't tell up from down; the world around me began to look like formless shapes and colors and a high-pitched buzz. No, not a high-pitched buzz—it was *the* high-pitched buzz. The same one that I heard—that all of us heard just the other night—when I saw those green eyes looking at us from the water.

"Guys! You there?" I called out, but the sound was so loud that I barely heard the words leave me.

I tried to focus on the ground in front of me, to find some kind of reference point for reality. The only thing that stood out from the mess of brown that was the island floor was a splotch of yellow. My eyes strained as I covered my ears to try and block out the noise and concentrate, and eventually I was able to make it out. It was a shoe, a yellow canvas show, sprayed with flecks of red, brown, and black.

Part of me wanted to reach down and pick it up, but another part of me begged that I not uncover my ears. The only sounds I could hear were the buzzing and my rapid heartbeat, pounding away like a brass drum inside my skull. I forced my eyes shut and shook my head back and forth, hoping I could thrash the noise away when a new sound came cutting through the buzzing. A growl—a deep, wet, guttural growl—and it was close.

I opened my eyes slowly and saw a hole in the ground about eight feet in front of me. It was wide, about the size of a two person canoe, and blanketed in the shade of the tall pines above. There was mud and lake scum draped around it, as well as a few misplaced fractals of yellowing bones. My heart began to slow, and I felt a voice in my head say, 'This is it' as my eyes met a pair of huge green eyes staring back at me from the darkness.

My legs began to move on their own, pedaling backwards as quickly as I could, and a bloodcurdling scream burst from my mouth. I turned to run full speed for the beach, and I could see through the trees that the boat was loaded and Levi was motioning to me to get on. The panic was the only thing I had to fuel me, and I ran like hell, feeling like whatever belonged to those eyes was on my heels. As soon as I had one foot on the boat, Barry floored it, almost knocking me back off. I'm still convinced that if Levi hadn't held onto me, I would have met my end right there, in the shallows of that terrible island.

The buzzing began to pass, leaving only the sound of the boat's engine in high gear and my breathing. "Did you guys see what it was? That, that, thing that chased me?" I looked around the boat for some sign of recognition but saw only blank stares. "Well?"

"I only saw the shape of it." Rodney said, looking at me, but his eyes were elsewhere, replaying the memory. "It looked big, real big."

"You know, when my Pops was stationed in Louisiana, we saw crocodiles all the time." Diego said, speaking fast. "Maybe it was a gator or something. Some oversized lizard thing."

"Crocodile or alligator?" Barry asked, sounding much more calm than us as he piloted the boat.

"Does it matter?" Levi shouted. "Nothing like that could survive in Nebraska. We have winter here, remember?"

"Well, what was it then?" Rodney shouted back. "What'd you see, Eddie?"

"I, uh, I don't know. It happened so fast that I didn't get a good look at it. All I saw were it's eyes." The image of them burned in my memory.

"Big green ones?" Dexter asked. "Like we saw the other night."

"Yeah, and there was the buzzing too." I tried to recall exactly what it sounded like, but found nothing in my experience that I could compare it to. "It was so loud. Did you hear it too?"

Everyone on board nodded, but only Barry knew what it was. "When it happened the other night, I thought it was a change in barometric pressure. Sudden changes in weather can cause your blood pressure to rise, and that can make your ears ring." He looked up at the sky for a moment and scanned the trees on the shore. "But there's no sign of a storm rolling in now."

"The fuck is barometric pressure?" Diego asked.

"Change in air pressure, basically. But like I said, I don't see anything coming in now, but I had that same feeling from the other night." Barry started to slow the boat. The covered dock was in view.

"So you're saying I almost got eaten by a gator that can survive winter and change the weather?" I asked.

"I mean, that could be a theory. All I'm saying is that the buzzing I heard sounded like the buzzing I hear when a storm rolls in." He stopped the boat, hopped out, and tied it off.

Levi didn't hesitate to start moving trash bags to the dock, like he wanted to keep his mind busy with something else. "The stories can't be true. It could have been a badger or something like that. There's just no way the stories are true."

"Like I said, there's a lot of stories here, would it be so crazy if one of them were true?" Barry said as he began to unload some of the tools we'd brought.

"Barry, do you hear yourself?" He yelled with a touch of a growl in his voice; that was the first showing of true anger we'd seen from Levi. "You know what? Just forget it. The only thing that matters is that no one tells Downs. It'll only complicate things."

"No one tells me what?" Downs was standing at the head of the path.

I Can't Swim

We all tried to come up with some story or excuse that would satisfy Downs' curiosity, but he'd heard us recounting what'd happened from a ways away and specifically heard the word 'gator' more than once. Levi tried to convince him that I'd only gotten spooked by a badger or something like that, but even the idea of a badger being on the island concerned him. Downs made it clear that if there was something on the island that could cause any sort of threat to camp, he was going to deal with it.

"Sir, please don't worry about it. I'll have the situation under control. I'm sure we're all just overreacting." Levi took one final stab at easing his concern.

"Mr. White, how old were you when you started coming here as a camper?" Downs wrapped his arm around Levi's shoulder.

"I think I was ten, sir."

"And in all the years you came here, you heard stories about some sort of lake monster, right?"

"Yes, sir, but that doesn't mean..."

"Shh, hear me out. Do you think it's possible, even in the slightest, that some small brood of animals could be living on that rock, perpetuating such ideas?"

"Well, I suppose that's possible."

"Alright then, I'm going to take a look." He let go of Levi and looked at me and the others. "Eddie, you'll be coming with me while the rest of you will accompany Mr. White to the gymnasium. The air conditioning has been acting up this morning, and I need you to take a look at it."

"Why's Eddie staying behind?" Dexter asked, showing a his disdain for me. "He's not getting a day off for getting too scared now, is he?"

Dexter let out a dry laugh that Diego cut short with a jab to his ribs. "Shut it."

"That's enough." Levi barked without looking back at us. "All of you, grab the bags from the boat and head up to camp."

I stood back and let the others do what they were told. My friends each looked at me with lost eyes as they left the dock and headed up the path. Levi and Downs exchanged a few words about what exactly needed to be done at the gymnasium before Levi went on his way too. Downs did not say anything to me until he was confident that the others were out of earshot.

"Well, Eddie, how do you feel about hunting?" He cracked a smile that made me squirm.

We walked together back to camp and to his office, all with him behind me, badgering me with questions about what I'd seen and how sure I was about what I'd seen. Something in the back of my mind told me not to tell him about the jawbone and shoe. I grew up in a house where you didn't stand trial for a mistake, you just went right to sentencing, so I guess I was worried I'd be pinned for something I didn't do.

When we emerged from the woods and started to make our way across the grounds, I noticed a commotion in the common area outside the mess hall. At least a dozen campers were huddled together and hollering at a pair of councilors who were standing on a picnic table, trying to quiet the crowd. The campers were all in their swimsuits and soaking wet, like they'd just run out of water.

"What happened there?" I asked and pointed to the crowd.

"No idea." Downs shrugged. "But if they need my help, they'll come find me."

We kept walking while I wondered what could have gotten so many people worked up enough to form a small mob. I didn't have to wonder for long.

"Honey, I hear you, but just because you think you saw something doesn't mean you did." Nurse Linda's voice roared out when Downs opened the door to the office cabin.

"I'm not crazy!" Kaya screamed back at her.

Kaya Smit was sitting in the nursing station with a towel and three blankets wrapped around her. Nurse Linda was there with her signature big hair, trying to take her temperature, and she looked like she'd about run her limit for the day. When Downs and I stepped through the door, her head snapped to look at us with eyes of desperation.

"Linda, what in the world is going on in here?" Downs asked while walking to his desk.

"While you were out on your little nature hike, we had a camper almost drown. That's what." Linda was at his desk with both hands leaning toward him in a heartbeat. "Why in the blazes didn't you answer your radio?"

Downs opened a drawer, pulled out a black radio, and placed it in front of her. "Left it here. I told you I was going on a hike to get away from work. I didn't want to bring it with me."

I'd known Nurse Linda to be a boisterous but patient person in our history together, but that day was the first day I saw her lose her cool.

"You incompetent fuckin' shitbird!" She pushed herself off the desk with enough force to knock it toward Downs and headed for the door. "You try running a camp full of kids without a nurse for a while. I'm taking a drive."

"Oh Linda, don't be like that. Where would you even go?" He stood up but stopped short of chasing after her.

"If I'm lucky, a bar and a young man's bed." She slammed the door behind her hard enough to shake the cabin.

Kaya and I shared a shocked look, and then the primal desire to impress the girl took over my mind. "You're running a tight ship here, Lester. Really. I'm sure anyone who saw that would be speechless."

He groaned and fell into his desk chair. "Go sit over there. I've got to call the Park Service and see what my options are."

"You have to call them about getting a new nurse?" Kaya asked.

"What? No." His desk phone was already raised to his head. "I've got to find out their policy on alligators." He swiveled his chair, turning his back to us.

"Did he say alligator?" She looked even more shocked than when Linda stormed out.

"It's a long story." I sat next to her on the bench I'd found myself on after Dexter tried to rearrange my face. "What happened to you?"

She laughed a bit. "It's also a long story."

Downs groaned again. "Yeah, I can hold. But can you at least tell them it's urgent?"

"Seems like we got time." I tried to crack a coy smile, but I was worried I just looked like a stroke victim.

Kaya laughed a bit more, then went on. "I'm not sure. All I know is that something pulled me under. Nurse Linda said it was a current that got me twisted around, but I don't think so."

I remembered the crowd of campers outside. "So the mob out there, you got something to do with that?"

She looked at her feet and tucked her chin in. The way a little kid does when they're embarrassed. "Yeah. Someone had to fish me out and give me CPR. It was a whole thing."

"Holy shit!" I nearly yelled.

"Shhhh." Downs craned his neck around his chair to look at me. "I'm on the phone."

"Sorry." I half whispered to him before looking back at Kaya. "Was something pulling you down? Or did you get caught on something?"

"I think so, but it could have been my fault too. I'm not a big fan of water. Well, actually, I can't swim."

"You can't swim?"

"No, I just never got around to learning, but I still love to go out on the kayaks. I was wearing a vest, but when the boat got turned over, I just never found my way back up." Her face went flat. "Something was pulling me. Something solid wrapped around my foot."

Kaya's eyes focused on the ground in front of her, and she began to speak softly, almost like she was talking to herself.

"Some of the boys in Cabin E have been bugging my friends and me since camp started, and today they challenged us to a race. We were supposed to paddle out to one of the old buoys and back. Camila tried to talk me out of doing it, but

I hate being shown up, so I told her I wasn't backing down. Her and Missy were with me, and it was going great, we were winning. I felt like we were miles ahead of them, and then right before we rounded the buoy, we hit something."

She looked up and leveled her eyes right into mine.

"When I looked down to see what it was, I saw those big green eyes Downs mentioned in his story, and they rushed up at me. The next thing I knew, the boat turned over, and I was being pulled down." Kaya looked away from me and refocused her stare on the ground. "If it hadn't been for Camila diving after me, I could have drowned."

"She was able to get you back to shore?"

Kaya shook her head back and forth. "No, but she got me to the surface. The boys we were racing with must have pulled up just in time. Missy said that they took me back to shore, and then Olivia had to give me CPR, and then, I guess, Nurse Linda showed up. I don't know." She sighed and looked at me with a hint of embarrassment in her eyes. "The whole thing was just a mess."

Downs slammed the phone down on his desk, causing both of us to jolt a bit. Personally, I'd forgotten he was there.

"This is taking too damn long." He glared at us. "Kaya, are you still in need of medical attention?"

She looked at me for insight; I could only shrug in response, so she stood up and said, "Guess not. Is that my queue to leave?"

"Yes ma'am. And if you could get the gathering of angry young folks to disperse, I'd be eternally grateful."

Kaya put her hand on my head and tussled my hair. "Catch you later, Eddie."

I'd wanted to say 'Yeah, you too', but I only managed to say, "Yeah, dude. Stay loose." I don't miss the feeling of getting tongue-tied around girls.

"Real smooth, Mr. Matthews." Downs quipped once she was out the door. "You know anything about hunting?"

Truthfully, I didn't know much, but I knew enough to talk shop. I'd taken hunter safety courses and pegged a few white tails, but I never got over my unease around dead things. Dad told me I'd outgrow it one day, but that day never seemed to come, so I never dug deeper into the subject than what I needed to know to survive an October hunting trip with my dad and uncle.

"I know enough. Why?"

He stood from his desk and walked over to a cabinet mounted on the wall opposite me. There was a large ring of keys that he kept on his belt at all times, and he fumbled with it for a minute before he found what he needed, unlocked the cabinet, and pulled out two revolver pistols. I was no gun expert, but from what I did know, I could tell they weren't meant for small game.

"You keep guns at a youth camp?" I didn't bother to hide my concern.

Downs looked at me with a raised eyebrow. "Of course. What if there was a bear?"

"In Nebraska? The last time anyone saw a bear here, it was in the seventies."

"You never know." He tucked one gun into his belt, behind his back, and put the other one in a small drawstring back on his desk. "You're going to take me down there and show me what you saw." Downs slid the bag on and headed for the door. "Come one, we're burning daylight."

"I really don't think that's a good idea."

He groaned and rubbed his forehead. "Listen, if there's something out on that island that's threatening the camp, it needs to be dealt with. I know that whatever you saw scared you half to death, but whatever it was can be explained. All I want you to do is ride out there with me and show me this..." Downs searched for the word. "This burrow that you found. Can you help me with that?"

I was going to tell him to fuck off and that I wasn't going back there because the thought of it made my skin want to crawl right off my body, but I didn't get the chance.

The phone rang, and Lester walked back to his desk in a huff and picked it up. "Yeah? Uh-huh. Well, I understand that. Sure. Sure. Alright, that works." He hung up and shifted his irritated gaze toward me. "I hope you're in the mood for bullshit."

Some Daylight Left

Someone from the park ranger's office had finally called Downs back and wanted more information. Luckily for them and unlucky for me, I was the firsthand witness and was expected to relay everything I'd experienced to whichever poor sap got stuck with the assignment. And what a poor sap he was.

"Pleasure to meet you both." A short, scrawny man stuck out his hand to introduce himself. "I'm Ranger Murphy, but everyone calls me Murph."

Murph was dressed in standard Ranger fare, a brown button-up shirt with two breast pockets, deep green shorts, hiking boots, and a wide-brimmed hat that made him look like he was trick-or-treating as a Camp Snoopy cartoon. He wore thin wire-framed glasses that sat on an oversized nose that almost resembled a beak, and behind his lenses was a pair of beady dark eyes. When Downs took his hand and shook it, Murph's whole body shook with it, like a child throttling a doll as they ran across their backyard. None of this instilled confidence in me.

"So I hear you guys have some sort of animal problem?" Murph asked as he took a seat.

Downs had agreed to meet with someone in the mess hall, since the camp was between meals, to go over a few questions the Rangers had. When we walked in, Murph was already there, which was odd, but no more odd than a lake monster possibly existing or finding a cashbox in an empty shed on an island no one ever goes to, so I didn't bother bringing it up. Instead, I went along, took my seat, and waited for Murph to tell Downs he was nuts.

"Something like that. To be honest, I haven't seen the thing, but Mr. Matthews here claims to have seen it firsthand." Downs slapped me on the back. "Go on, tell Ranger Murphy here what you told me."

Murph looked at me and cracked a smile that I think was meant to make me feel comfortable, but only made me squirm. "I can't say for sure what I saw. For all I know, it was just a hole."

"Alright, well, let's start with the basics." Murph pulled out a pocket notebook and pen and opened it to a new page. "Did you see a creature of any kind while you were on the island?"

"I saw something, but I didn't get a good enough look at it to see what it was."

"Fair enough. Let's focus on the hole, then. Director Downs had mentioned on the phone that you came across some kind of nest or burrow; is that true?"

"It was a hole, a good-sized one, sitting between a few of the trees out there. From what I could see, it was deep and big enough that I could have slipped into it if I wasn't paying attention."

"I see." Murph started jotting down notes on his pad. "Did you see any signs of animal life?"

"Couldn't say. I wasn't really looking for any. The only thing I saw that seemed animal-like was, well, I paused and wondered how to phrase it. "I saw something that looked like a set of eyes in the hole, looking up at me, then they seemed to lunge, so I ran."

"What kind of eyes?"

"What kind of eyes?" Downs questioned with the same tone my mother used when she wanted me to feel stupid. "What kind of question is that? He said they were eyes! You want to know if they were bat eyes or skunk eyes? Is that it?"

Murph looked at me with raised eyebrows. "Could you do that?"

"No." I surprised myself with how annoyed I sounded. "They were eyes—green eyes, big green eyes. Alright? That's what I got."

"Right...." Murph tapped his pen on the table for a moment while he thought. "What were you doing on the island?"

Downs' face froze at the question, likely worrying about getting hit with a fine for not maintaining the island, like Levi had pointed out. "We were doing some cleanup. Part of the maintenance work."

Murph looked puzzled. "Aren't you a camper here? Why are you doing maintenance work?"

"Oh, right." I placed a hand on Downs' shoulder. "Lester here put me and my friends on maintenance duty after I got punched in the face right after registration. He was worried I might be a bad egg, even though I was the victim. Ain't that right, Lester?"

"Now just hold on a second." He brushed my hand off of him. "It ain't like that."

"Lester?" Murph wrote the name down. "May I call you that, Lester?"

"No." Downs leaned back in his chair. "You may not."

"Fair enough." Murph stood up from the table and put away his notepad. "Can you show me this burrow?"

Again, I have no idea why I blindly followed Downs and Ranger Murphy, but I did. We crossed the camp and drew the attention of confused onlookers as we went. Some kids just watched; others pointed and asked questions aloud like 'Is he getting kicked out?' and 'Who called the tree cop?', but most only lent us a puzzled expression before moving on to something more interesting. I envied them—all the kids who got to be regular campers while I was stuck chasing skunks, repairing docks, and getting sucked into folk tales I didn't want to believe in.

When we finally made it to the covered dock, the sun was on its descent toward the horizon, but that didn't stop Murph.

"We got some daylight left, best we make this quick." He stepped aboard the boat after Downs and me and he insisted on piloting the boat.

The boat rolled across the lake's still waters with ease while Murph and Downs debated what I could have seen. I didn't catch what they were saying, at least not the details of it, because I was listening for something. As soon as the boat pulled into open water, I thought I heard it again, but it was hard to tell. Then the island came into view, and then the details came into shape, and there was no debating it. The buzzing sound was still in the air.

Only a shred of daylight was left at that point, and the sky was painted in hues of pink and orange, meaning night wasn't far off.

"There's no point in going ashore if we can't see what we're dealing with." Downs said, sounding a bit defeated.

"I agree, but I'd get hell from the others at the station if I went back empty-handed." Murph added, sounding the sternest he'd been since we met. "No one's going to get hurt from taking a quick peek."

He started to pilot the boat closer to shore while Downs continued to demand he turn around, saying that if there was some man-eating thing, he didn't want to face it in the dark, but Murph insisted we'd be fine. Before the boat cut into the rocky shallows, something caught my eye in the last slivers of light at the bend of the island. At first, I thought it was a log, but the shape of it was too uniform, so I asked. "Do you guys see that?"

Both of them looked to where I was pointing, and Murph shone his flashlight at the shape and revealed a kayak. The cheap, brightly colored yellow plastic kind you could get from most big box stores was tied down to a fallen tree and gently bobbed in the water. He moved the light along the rope that tethered it to the shore until a pair of boot tracks revealed themselves on the beach.

"It seems we have company." Downs said, as he felt for the pistol he'd tucked into his waistband.

"Who'd come out here at this time of night?" Murph asked.

Using the flashlight beam, Murph followed the tracks to the island's treeline, and we could see the glinting of the shack's tin roof in the distance. "What in the world is that?"

"It looks like a, uh," Downs squinted at it while my stomach tied itself into a knot. "A building or shed." He looked back at me. "Did you boys come across any buildings out here?"

Part of me knew there was no point in lying; eventually, they'd go ashore and find the shack for themselves, but the other part of me wanted to keep my guard up and keep Downs in the dark. I knew that they'd be lucky to find the cashbox in the dirt without my help, but there was still a chance that Downs would find it and turn it in, or worse, claim it as camp property. I settled on a half-truth.

"Yeah, an old shed. It just has some old tools in it, though; nothing too weird about it. Other than being out here by itself." I could feel a nervous heartbeat in my throat as I answered him.

"Odd. I don't remember there being anything on this dirt mound." Downs looked back toward the island with a furrowed brow.

"Nothing on any of the maps either. At least not that I've seen." Murph added. "We should check it out."

As Murph reached for the boat's throttle, the low buzzing that had filled the air spiked into a high-pitched ringing. I instinctively reached to cover my ears and saw Down and Murph do the same. The pair of them shot each other a panicked glance before looking at me.

"What is this?" Murph asked, almost yelling over the noise in his head.

"I don't know." I hollered. "It happened before too."

Before any of us could get our bearings, a new sound rolled out into the night air: a loud, wet growl—the kind of growl that you just know in your soul belongs to something much more dangerous than yourself. The three of us looked back to the island just in time to see something large and dark slide into the water, and a pair of bright green orbs appeared just below the lake's surface. I froze. I wanted to tell them to turn the boat around and get away from there as quickly as possible, but I froze.

"What, in the name of Mary and Joseph, is that?" Murph yelled, pointing toward the orbs.

Downs dove from the rear of the boat to the pilot's seat, pushing Murph out of the way as he did. He took hold of the helm in one hand and threw the throttle forward with the other, forcing the boat into a U-turn away from the island and back toward open water. The boat moved with enough force that it knocked me out of my frozen state and sent me toppling to the floor.

"What are you doing?" Murph screamed while getting to his feet. "We can't just leave. There's a job to do."

"Not in the dark, no sir, not in the dark." Downs said this with his eyes fixed straight ahead and his knuckles white with pressure. "Whatever that is, it's a daylight kind of problem, you understand?"

A battle of wills broke out then, even though Murph didn't dare to take control of the ship back by force. Downs had about a foot and 80 pounds on him, and it showed. They bickered about the ethics of leaving the creature free for another night and whether or not they should be concerned about the mystery person on the island, but I tuned them out again. My ears were focused on the buzzing, still ringing high and loud in my head, and my eyes were fixated on the green spheres trailing the boat, staring up at me.

I hadn't realized that I'd started leaning over the railing at the boat's rear when Murph yelled, "Eddie! Be..."

His words were cut off by the roar of water replacing my atmosphere.

We'd hit a crossing wave, just big enough to knock me overboard, leaving me in the water. Everything in me told me to swim up, to find air, to fight to survive—but all of that seemed so unimportant when I saw those lights approaching. They didn't rush; they seemed to take their time, they just inched closer and closer as I stared back. And when they were close enough, there was no denying it; I was staring back into an intelligent set of eyes.

Sure You Do

I should have been panicked, terrified, or anything other than what I was—hypnotized. The eyes that stared back at me were nearly the size of my head and glowed with a deep green hue that had streaks of calm blue in their foreground. It's iris was wide and seemed to pierce through me as it stared. Whatever the eyes belonged to was shrouded in the chilled darkness of the water, but I was able to make out something narrow and lightly colored, like a horn or tusk, nestled between the eyes that had me stuck in that trance.

My chest began to ache, and I watched my already limited vision begin to darken. I told myself to move, to swim upward, but I was stuck, unable to look away from the eyes that were getting closer and closer. The only thing I could think to do was scream, but I couldn't even manage that. As far as I could tell, I was either going to drown or be eaten by whatever was lurking toward me.

I'd just allowed the thought of death to sink in when I heard two loud cracking sounds from somewhere above me, followed by a gurgled screech from whatever thing was in the water with me. The eyes that had me frozen darted toward the surface and hurried upward. My body became mine again, and I tried with all my might to swim up for air, but my lungs were depleted and my brain had started playing visions of my life. It was too late for me to save myself, or at least it seemed to be.

I've replayed that moment every which way I could, and I still am not sure what happened next. There was a clamoring sound at the surface above me, like splashing, yelling, and cracking noises all formed into one out-of-tune synompny, and then there was a tugging feeling in my chest. Like something was pulling me toward it, like the way a magnet pulls a paperclip, but I'm not sure which direction it was being pulled in.

The next clear memory I have is of waking up in the nurses station to the sound of Nurse Linda's voice going a mile a minute. "I leave you alone for one day, one godforsaken day, and you go and throw this young man off a boat."

I was lying on the cold vinyl table she insisted on propping all the injured kids up on with my eyes glued to the yellowed ceiling tiles above me. It seemed best to lie still and not speak.

"For Christ sake, Lester, what were you thinking?" She continued.

Murph's voice, more frail than it was before, came to Downs defense. "To be fair, ma'am, he was accompanied by a park ranger. I assure you, I wouldn't have let any harm fall upon them."

"Don't get me started with you." I could hear the rage in Linda's voice. "I've sseen dandelions tougher than you, and you did let him get hurt! Poor Eddie here almost drowned while you two were off hunting for make-believe alligators."

"Crocodile, actually." Downs muttered from deeper in the room. I still didn't dare to move.

"Excuse me." Linda hissed.

"We think it's a crocodile, Linda, not an alligator." Down spoke up. "And if you'd calm down for a fuckin' second, maybe we'd be able to tell you what happened out there. Right Murph?"

"Well, I, uh, you see." The frail Ranger danced with his words for a second. "To be clear, I don't think it's a crocodile or an alligator. Officially speaking, until a sample can be collected, it is simply considered an anomaly."

"I don't give a rat's ass what you think it is, or what you call it. The point is, you two yahoo's almost got this boy killed." Linda hit the table I was lying on to make her point, causing me to jump a bit, giving away that I was awake. "Oh! I'm so sorry, Eddie. How are you feeling?"

Linda fell right back into her healing rhythm, sitting me up, checking my pulse with her hand, feeling my forehead for a temperature, and shining a light in my eyes and ears.

"I'm okay, I guess." I answered while she went through her mental checklist. "What happened to me?"

She didn't answer; she only gave me a look that sat somewhere between concern and pity.

"Linda, Murph, could you give us the room, please?" Lester asked from behind his desk.

"Are you joking? I'm not leaving you alone with this boy again." Linda grabbed my head and pulled me in for an uncomfortable side squeeze.

Murph had been sitting at one of the unused desks before standing up and pulling a pair of handcuffs out of one of the compartments on his belt. "I'm sorry about this, Director Downs, but Linda is right."

"What's this about, Murph?" Downs pushed his chair away from his desk and stood up.

"It's Ranger Murphy from now on." He walked up to Downs desk and placed the handcuffs in front of him. "When we got back, I stopped by my truck and radioed the station. I was curious what a camp director was doing with two firearms on his person, and it turns out you don't have a license to carry."

Downs' eyes widened. "Now come one, there's no need to make a mountain out of a molehill, right? We clearly have other issues at play here. I'm sure we can work out something, right, Murph? I mean, Ranger Murphy."

Murph took off his oversized hat, ran his hand through his thinning hair, and put it back on. "Afraid not, Lester. I called for backup in the truck; they should be here any minute. You're looking at two unsilenced firearms charges and discharging a weapon without a license on federal land. You can trust us to handle your mystery animal, but clearly you can't be trusted to keep the campers here safe."

"Holy shit." The words fell out of me.

"Holy shit is right," Linda said as she finally let go of me.

At first, I thought Downs would do what most people would do in that situation: surrender, but then I caught a glimmer of something in his eye. I wondered if it was determination or maybe fear, but it became clear quickly that it was resistance. Downs pulled his gun out of his waistband and put it on the table in front of it, with the muzzle pointed toward Murph, and then took off his drawstring bag that held the other gun. He placed that one on the desk, off to his right.

"You ever play cowboys as a kid, Ranger?" The words slid smoothly from Downs tongue. "Were you ever the quickest to draw?"

"Lester, what on earth are you getting at?" Linda stood up, but stopped short of approaching the desk.

"Linda," Murph spoke softly. "Please stay where you are with Mr. Matthews." Murph took a shaky hand and placed it on his holster. "I have the situation under control."

"Sure you do, Ranger." Downs smirked. "You know I served for 12 years in the Navy. Carrying that weapon like yours makes you feel like a big man, don't it? But you know what? You never think you're going to have to use it, do you?"

"Lester, step away from the desk with your hands up." Murph didn't flinch, but I could see sweat starting to pour out of him. "I won't ask twice."

My eyes started darting between the gun on the desk, the bag with the other gun, and both of their faces. I'd never been witness to a standoff before. I was a kid from flyover country, and strange things happened a lot, just not that kind of strange. Linda seemed stuck, and the others seemed like they were heading to a proper shootout. For some reason, I felt like I had to do something.

"Lester, did you get a good look at it?" I blurted out as I jumped to my feet. "The thing that chased us."

He kept his face fixed toward Murph, but let his eyes wander to mine. "What are you doing?"

"I want to know if you saw it. Was it as big as you thought it was? Did you see it's eyes?"

"It's eyes?" He hissed the question at me.

"Yeah, the eyes." I dared to take a few steps forward, until I was past Linda. "When I got pulled under, I saw them floating toward me. I wasn't sure what they were at first, but once they were close enough, there was no doubting it; they were eyes. Big green eyes."

"I did see something green. But they seemed too bright to be real." He turned his head to face me too. "Are you sure they were eyes?"

"Eddie, what are you doing?" Murph kept his gaze on downs and his hand on his holster. I wanted to wink or something to let him know I was on his side, but I was too nervous to try to be coy.

"We went out there to find that thing, right? And we found it. So what do we think it is?" I could feel a nervous ache start to form in my chest.

"It was too big to be an alligator." Downs' body language started to relax. "But it swam like one. I was sure I saw a tail, a huge tail, pushing it along."

"Really?" I dared to take another step closer. "I saw something between its eyes when it got close to me. Maybe a horn or snout. Whatever it was, it was pretty big and sat right between its eyes."

"Eddie, why don't you let Director Downs and I talk alone?" Murph asked sternly, his gaze still on Downs.

"You know, Lester." I paused to swallow a mouthful of panic. "We aren't going to be able to find this thing if the camp becomes a crime scene. You understand that, right?"

Downs shifted his gaze back to Murph, leaned forward, and placed his hand a few inches away from the bag. "Then our dear friend here only needs to leave peacefully."

"I can't do that. You're clearly not okay, Lester." Murph's eye twitched from how hard he was staring.

"I'm only trying to do what's right!" Downs slammed his first down on his desk. "You don't understand. This isn't my first run-in with that thing, and it certainly won't be my last as long as I'm breathing. No, sir, my last dealing with that thing will be the day I kill it. You understand me?"

"The story on the beach, then, is it true? You've seen this thing before?"

"What are you two talking about?" Murph was starting to loose composer when we didn't answer him right away. His teeth chatted as he spoke. "I am an officer of the peace and you will answer me!"

Downs was distracted, but still on edge. I had to do something. "Lester, I'm sorry about this."

My hands started to move before I had commanded them to, and I snatched the drawstring bag from the desk. I slid the bag across the floor toward Linda, who still stood frozen. Downs started to let out a scream before reaching for the gun on the desk and raising it to Murph. Ranger Murphy did not raise his gun; instead, he fell backwards, covering his face with his hands.

Downs pulled the trigger repeatedly, but no shots rang out; only the clicking sound of an empty gun emitted from his grip. He looked at the gun, puzzled. "What the hell?"

Linda had somehow unfroze herself, whether by willpower or instinct, I'll never know, and had grabbed a metal tray from her nurses station. Before Downs could make sense of what was happening, she had lifted the tray and chucked it across the room toward him, knocking the gun out of his hand. He shot her a death glare, but was too late to act on it.

Ranger Murphy had scrambled back to his feet, drew his weapon, and demanded Downs surrender. He gave in at that time, though he wasn't quiet about it. Lester Downs insulted Nurse Linda and me with just about every unpleasant turn of phrase you could think of. Not that either of us gave him much thought; under the circumstances, we didn't think too kindly of him either.

Not even 10 minutes later, another truck from the Ranger station pulled up with its lights splashing red and blue through the night on its approach. The whole ordeal had gotten the attention of every camper and staff member, and all of them were present to watch the stoic Lester Downs be stuffed into the back of a truck and shipped out.

After Downs completed his perp walk, Rodney found me in the crowd. "Eddie, hol shit man, we've been looking for you everywhere."

"Yeah, sorry, Downs had me busy."

We watched as the truck pulled off with Downs in the back. "Not gonna lie, I got a ton of questions, but we got a problem first."

"What's wrong?" The idea that another thing had gone wrong didn't even phase me at that point.

"It's Diego. He's missing."

Unaccounted For

The councilors started to wrangle all the campers into the mess hall for an impromptu meeting of sorts, which included Rodney and me. On the way in, I filled him in on everything that had happened with Downs, Murph, the monster, the kayak and tracks on the island, and of course, the standoff in the office. To my surprise, he didn't question anything I told him. Rodney took it all at face value and went right back to telling me about Diego.

We found a table in the far corner with Barry, Dexter, and Kaya already sitting there. When we sat down, Barry asked, "Have you seen him, Eddie? Rodney told you about Diego, right?"

"And Megan, you remembered to mention her too, right, Rodney?" Kaya blurted.

"Hold on a minute." I shook my head and put my hands up in a stop motion. "Diego and Megan are missing?"

"It's probably nothing. For all we know they're just hiding out in the woods or something." Dexter said, leaning back on his chair and staring at the ceiling.

"Well, that answers that. They probably just ran off to play Russian roulette with an STD in the woods." I quipped, feeling a bit bad for the insult but not bad enough to not say it.

"That's what I'm saying." Dexter exclaimed, putting his chair back on the ground.

Kaya's face turned red with rage. "It's not funny. They've been missing all night, and no one can find them. If Megan was going to sneak out, she would have said something."

Barry looked at her skeptically. "Really? She would have said, 'Hey gals, just so you know, I'm going to sneak off and fuck Diego's brain out on a log. Be back in five.'? I don't think she would've."

Kaya's face warped from righteous anger to slight embarrassment. "Well, no, she wouldn't have said that. But I think she would've dropped a hint."

"How long have they been gone?" I asked, still thinking this was less important than the standoff I just survived.

"Hard to say, after we left you with Downs, Diego told Levi that he needed to stop by The Hole. He never caught up with us." Rodney answered, his legs shaking nervously under the table as he spoke.

"Weird. And Megan?"

"Sometime this afternoon. She said she had a headache and had to lie down. We didn't see her at dinner, and she wasn't in the cabin at lights out." Kaya answered. "Olivia and Levi have been looking for them for a while, but they still haven't come back."

"So we actually have four missing people?" My stomach sank at the thought of it.

We all shared a concerned glance; even Dexter looked worried. Our friends and part-time guardians had seemingly evaporated into the woods while there was a monster lurking in the lake—an equation for disaster. But disaster would have to wait.

Mrs. Leaver, the head cook who'd stuck me and Dexter in the dish pit together the first night, stood up on a table and banged together two pots to get the room's attention. Everyone hushed and looked up to her. She stood there for a minute, seeming to silently dare someone to make a noise, but no one did, and once she seemed satisfied, she spoke up.

"Thank you all for coming. I know there are many questions about Director Downs, but now isn't the time for questions, so I'll tell you what I can. Lester Downs has been taken into custody and will no longer serve as camp director. Until a new director is appointed, I'll be taking over his role to keep things moving smoothly. If any of you campers no longer feel the same here at Camp Alkali, I completely understand and am willing to work with your parents to issue refunds and arrange transport to get you home."

A small whisper began to wade through the tables of campers, and Mrs. Leaver waited for it to die down before continuing.

"With that being said, it's been brought to my attention that two campers have gone missing and may be in need of our help. Starting tomorrow morning, the Park Rangers will be here and are welcoming the assistance of volunteers in a search with them through the outer grounds. If you are able and willing, please report to the camp office at seven tomorrow morning. Until then, I ask everyone to return to your cabin and try to get some rest."

We didn't even have a chance to debate if we should leave or hang around when someone snuck up from behind me and put a hand on my shoulder. "Edward Matthews?" A female voice asked.

My body jumped a bit, and I whipped my head toward whoever it was. She was a short woman in a Park Rangers uniform, with densely freckled cheeks and the look of pure exhaustion etched into her face. I hesitated to answer, wondering if I had done something to warrant my own ride out of camp, which made me squint and ask again.

"Edward Matthews, correct?" She practically hissed.

"Eddie. Folks call me Eddie."

She nodded. "Alright, I need you to wait here. We have some questions for you."

"We?"

"Yes, we." She looked at the others at the table. "Y'all stay here too, just in case."

Mrs. Leaver dismissed the campers and staff back to their lodgings, and we waited as they all shuffled out the mess hall's steel double doors. My friends and I shared a few concerned glances as we wondered what the Rangers could need all of us for. Even Dexter looked like he was sweating a little, and he had become a master in the art of looking like you don't give a shit, even when you truly do. That is not a quality I recommend tolerating in people.

Once the room was empty and the stiff quiet of night had settled back into the room, Mrs. Leaver, Nurse Linda, and the freckled Park Ranger each took a seat at our table. The three of them seemed to be sending silent messages to each other, pleading for someone to start talking. But none of them dared to take the first step.

"You said you had some questions for us; is that right?" Kaya asked while placing her hands on the table, with her fingers interlocked together. Like she was starting off a business meeting.

Mrs. Leaver cleared her throat and placed her hands on the table, just like Kaya had. "I know that tonight has been quite, um, stressful, especially for you, Eddie."

"Oh, yes," Nurse Linda cut in. "This poor boy deserves a medal for what he did. The bravest soul I've ever come across, I can tell you that."

"Right, and we are forever thankful for that. But something else has come to our attention." Mrs. Leaver turned her focus to me. "Eddie, did you happen to see anyone out on the water tonight when you were out with Lester and Ranger Murphy?"

I felt all eyes fall on me, and my nerves kicked in. My frazzled brain focused on the words 'out on the water' and we hadn't seen anyone on the water, but I forgot to mention the kayak and tracks on the island. "Not that I remember, but to be honest, it's been a long night."

"I understand." Mrs. Leaver gave a forced smile to mask her weary disappointment.

"Is this about Diego and Megan?" Rodney asked. "Cause we haven't seen this since this afternoon."

The three adults looked at each other again and silently begged the others to take the lead. It took about thirty seconds, but the Ranger took the lead. "We're aware that they are unaccounted for, yes."

"What about Levi and Olivia? Did they ever come back?" Kaya asked, her hands still sitting on the table like they were made of stone.

"Well, uh, maybe we should get acquainted first." The Ranger took her hat off and placed it on the table. "I'm Ranger Griner, but most people just call me Sabrina."

Barry cut her off, which was unusual for the laid-back Barry. "Alright, Sabrina, what are you not telling us?"

Sabrina looked stunned for a moment before setting her gaze squarely on the hat that sat in front of her. "Did either Levi or Olivia have any—let's call it bad blood—between them?"

"What? No." Dexter said. "They were totally into each other. Honestly, it was gross."

"Interesting." Sabrina muttered.

"Mrs. Leaver, please just tell us what happened." The words came out of me sounding more like a demand than a request.

She ran her hands through her thinning hair and sighed. "Olivia's body was recovered by Ranger Griner not long before Ranger Murphy radioed into the station about the situation with Lester."

"Oh my god." Kaya said, sounding like she'd had the wind knocked out of her.

"No fucking way." Dexter gasped. "No. Fucking. Way."

"Mind your manners, young man." Linda scolded. "It's shocking, yes, but we don't need to stain her memory with your poor choice of words."

"I'm sorry. I just, oh god, I'm sorry." He sank into his chair.

"We don't have a cause of death yet. The county coroner will have to take a look at her, but he's not available for a couple days." Sabrina added. "But that means that Levi, Diego, and Megan are all still unaccounted for."

Her whole demeanor bothered me. She looked robotic almost, with a stiff back, squared shoulders, and a tight jaw whenever she didn't speak. I couldn't tell if she was just a poor conversationalist or if she truly was a few marbles short. Either way, it was starting to irritate me.

"Why do you keep saying that? Unaccounted for. They're missing, right? So we should be calling the sheriff right about now, don't you think?" I leaned forward as I spoke, making sure she understood I was serious, not that I expected her to care.

Sabrina shifted a bit, breaking her robotic composure. "It's just the term they train us to use. They say it helps family and friends stay focused on the facts. I didn't mean to make it sound like I wasn't taking this matter seriously."

"Oh." I felt a tad of guilt, but not enough to make me change my demeanor much. "Well then, what are we going to do about it?"

"There's not much that can be done tonight." Mrs. Leaver took charge of the conversation. "But tomorrow more Rangers and a few deputies will want to talk to you. A search is planned, but given what happened tonight, we don't want them anywhere near the camp grounds." She panned across all of our faces, trying to read our thoughts and make sure we were understanding her. "The last thing anyone needs is campers who are more concerned than they already are. So tonight I need you to go back to your cabins, sit tight, and wait for someone to fetch you in the morning. We plan on meeting down by the staff dock. I understand you boys already know where that is."

Rodney, Dexter, and I nodded.

"Good. Kaya, Linda can show you the way in the morning." She stood up, and the other two followed her lead. "Go get some sleep, and please don't wander off. There's enough to deal with already."

"Would it be too much trouble to have someone walk me back to my cabin?" Kaya asked, still sounding like she was recovering from a gut punch.

"I can." The words blurted out of me, not sounding subtle at all.

"You've done more than your share of good deeds tonight, Mr. Matthews." Linda gave me a warm smile and a knowing look. "I'll walk you back, sweetheart, don't you worry."

The walk from the mess hall back to The Hole is a blurry spot in my memory, but I don't remember talking much. Looking back on it, I'm convinced that it must have been the first quiet moment I had since Lester placed his gun on the desk and challenged Murph to a shootout. My mind must have started to retreat into itself, only to be snapped out of its trance once we reached the front door of our cabin by one of Dexter's stupid remarks.

"I'm just saying it's a waste of good ass. She was hot. I get why Levi was drooling over her."

"Fuck you." Rodney said, yanking the door open and stepping inside. "The poor gal's dead, and you're thinking about how hot she was? The fuck is wrong with you?"

"You know what's funny? My mom asks me that question all the time." Dexter flopped into his bunk. "What do you think, Eddie? Would you've tapped that?"

"Go to hell." I climbed into my bunk and pulled my covers over my head. "Seriously, though, you're sick, Dexter."

"Yeah, yeah, yeah. Whatever you say." I could hear him smirking. It was weird how chipper Dexter suddenly seemed.

Sleep didn't come easy that night. I kept slipping into a dream where I saw a body floating in the water in front of me. It looked to be drifting from me, so I reached out to try to grab it, and then it's head shot up to look at me with the same deep green eyes that pulled me under. The images of that dream have never left me.

Eventually, I was shot awake by a slamming sound.

"Fuck! What was that?" I called out to the darkness of the cabin.

"I don't know." Barry said, sounding just as startled as I did. "Hit the lights."

Rodney scrambled from his bunk, flipped the light switch by the door, and surveyed the room. "Guys, where's Dexter?"

He wasn't in his bunk, so I peeked out the window next to my bed and saw a flashlight wandering in the dark toward the woods. "What is he doing?"

Canoe or Kayak?

If it had been under less suspicious circumstances, we probably wouldn't have cared that Dexter disappeared; hell, we might have even welcomed it. But after all the bizarre events of that day, we knew it meant he was up to something. The three of us jumped out of our bunks and rushed out the door to see what he was doing, but by then the only evidence of him being out there in the pitch-black was the fading beam of a flashlight bobbing down the footpath.

"Hey!" Rodney yelled. "Where the hell are you going?" His voice sliced through the night air, but Dexter didn't seem bothered—he just kept walking.

"Barry, what time is it?" I asked as I tried to piece together what Dexter could be up to too.

He checked his watch, rubbed his eyes, then checked it again to be sure. "A bit after three."

"In the morning?" Rodney sounded stunned.

All I could do was slam my palm against my forehead. "Obviously."

"Well, what's he doing taking a hike at three in the morning?" He defended himself.

I wasn't sure; I didn't even have a guess, but I figured it could only be a bad omen. "Come on. We need to follow him."

"You're joking, right?" Rodney asked, crossing his arms to show his resistance to the idea.

I went back inside and hurried to change into some clean clothes. My father insisted that I bring an oversized flashlight with me, so I grabbed it out of my back and slid my shoes on. Barry and Rodney stood in the doorway of the cabin with their jaws hung open, looking like preschoolers who had discovered chimpanzees at the zoo for the first time.

"Am I doing this alone?" I asked as I shoved past them and jumped down the rotting steps.

"I'm in." Barry went inside to get ready.

Rodney fidgeted where he stood for a moment. "I don't like this, Eddie. Something about it ain't on the up and up."

"I know." I assured him as I flicked my flashlight on and shined it down the path. "That's why we've got to do something about it."

He hung his head and turned inside, but not before muttering, "Fuck my life."

They rushed, just like I had, and fumbled down the cabin steps to where I waited. Both of them brought their own flashlight, though Barry's was more of an electric lantern, but it got the job done, and Rodney insisted on bringing his pocket knife while Barry insisted on bringing his flip phone. By the time we finally started to head down the footpath to the woods, we'd lost sight of Dexter's light.

We were approaching the tree line when Barry asked, "Any ideas where he's going?"

"The dock, maybe, to go steal that money for himself, I bet." Rodney sneered. "He's a rat, he's always has been and always will be."

"You can say that again." I added. "He's been a pain in my ass since the fourth grade. Every summer makes my life hell."

"Yeah, he's a jackass, but you think he'd be able to pilot the boat himself?" Barry asked, sounding surprising clear headed for the early hour. "I mean, I'm used to boats like that, but he'd probably have a hard time with it."

"That's a good point." I racked my brain for other places he would go, and then I remembered something. "When I went to the island with Downs and that Ranger, we saw a kayak out there."

"That was already there." Rodney said, swatting a bug from his face. "It was on the beach the first day we floated by, remember?"

I knew what he was talking about. When Levi first showed us the boat and the dock, we did a pass of the island and saw an overturned orange canoe wedged into the rocky beach. It looked like it'd been there for a while; for all I knew it was red before the sun faded its color. Not that it mattered; the point was that the boat wasn't the one I saw.

"The orange canoe? No, that wasn't it, I remember that. I saw a yellow kayak tied off on a log, and there were footprints on the beach leading away from it."

"Then where'd that one come from?"

"I don't know. Maybe it was those guys who robbed those gas stations Megan told us about. Maybe they took kayaks to the island to hide out or something."

"Canoe or kayak?" Barry asked.

"Does it matter?"

"Well, there's a difference."

"Barry, will you shut up and focus?" Rodney barked. "We've got bigger issues here."

I was going to come to Barry's defense but was interrupted by the sound of a voice echoing amongst the trees. We had just come up on the part of the path that slipped off toward the dock but didn't see any light. The three of us gave a nod, signaling it was time to shut up, and kept moving deeper down the path and further into the woods.

I was fairly certain it was the same path that Dexter had used to show us the lookout where we first spotted the island. Even with the combination of all of our flashlights, the woods still seemed so dark that I felt claustrophobic. The trees appeared to be glaring down at us, the path felt like it was thinning, and every toad croak and cricket song suddenly sounded like threats from the forest demanding that we turn tail and leave. We didn't listen.

We came up on the part of the path that was etched into my memory—the steep drop-off that overlooked the lake—the first time I saw those glowing green eyes in the water. That night, we all heard that paralyzing ringing in our ears, and we were hearing it again, just not as intense. It was like it was building toward something, low and steady but increasing just enough with every step to be noticeable. But the thing that really caught my attention was the voices, loud enough to be clearly heard here, echoing up from the bottom of the drop-off.

"I don't care, alright. What's done is done." The voice rang out.

All three of us switched our lights off and tried to peer over the edge. Just like before, it looked like the drop-off plummeted right into the lake, but as I built up the courage to get close to the edge, I could see a small strip of beach and a dim glowing light. My eyes tried to adjust to make out a shape, but I couldn't see anything clearly under the moonlight.

"That doesn't mean it was okay. We need to do something." Another voice rose from the beach below.

Barry patted me on the shoulder and pointed to something in the distance. "I think I see a way down."

It was hard to see in the dulling moonlight, but I thought I understood. There was a hill just around the bend that was dotted with pine trees. It was a steep hill but manageable. If we watched our steps and stayed close to each other, it'd get us closer to Dexter or whoever else was down on that beach.

Barry led the way, while Rodney and I did our best to follow his lead and match his steps. Once we had made it about halfway down the hill I noticed that the ringing had plateaued at an irritating frequency that made it feel like something had crawled inside my head and started buzzing. I did my best to ignore it and focus on the voices on the beach. With each step closer, the voices became more clear and distinct—so distinct that I was sure I knew the voice, just not well enough to name them.

The three of us hadn't discussed a plan on exactly how we'd approach Dexter once we found him or what we'd do with him, so it shouldn't have surprised me when Rodney took the lead.

We had just touched down on the strip of beach; the lights we'd seen on the ledge were maybe 10 yards ahead of us, and Rodney screamed out, "Dexter, have you lost your goddamn mind? Running out here in the middle of the night to meet up with who? What's going on?"

The lights flashed toward us, and a voice asked, "Rodney?" It clicked, and I knew who it was. "Why are you looking for Dexter?" It was Diego.

"Diego? Holy shit, you alright?" Barry ran past us toward him and nearly tackled him to the sand.

Rodney and I jogged after him, and as we got closer, we could see Diego pinned under Barry and a pissed-off-looking Megan sitting crossed-legged behind them.

"What are you two morons doing out here?" Rodney asked, not bothering to hide his anger. "The whole camp thinks you two ran off. The Park Rangers and Sheriff's Department are coming out here tomorrow to look for you."

"See!" Megan snarled and jumped to her feet. "I told you this was a stupid idea, but no, you couldn't listen to me, could you?"

Diego wrestled Barry off of him and scrambled to his feet. "My sweet flower, please believe me, I had no idea it'd all go so wrong."

"That's because you don't think." She shoved him in the chest and turned her back to him. "This is why I need a real man. Someone who can fix the shit they break."

"Oh my god, you're impossible!" Diego screamed loud enough to cause a flock of birds to evacuate somewhere nearby.

Barry stepped in between them and put one hand on Megan's back and the other on Diego's chest. "There, there. Trouble in paradise?"

They both took a step away from him.

"So what happened exactly?" I dared to ask, knowing full well I was inviting an earful from them both.

I got the earful I expected, and was able to break down their lists of complaints and conflicts into a story I was mostly able to follow. Diego found an old pedal boat behind the tool shed and hatched the idea of inviting Megan out for a private evening picnic on the island. Things went as planned at first; they snuck out while there was still daylight left, stole some food from the mess hall while the staff was setting up dinner, and made their way to the water. Everything would have gone great if Diego hadn't gotten lost.

It turned out that Diego had a shit sense of direction, and the island was so far from shore that he'd start wondering if the current had thrown him off course, and he'd start moving in a different direction. To make matters worse, once it was dark out, they noticed that the pedal boat had started to take on water from somewhere, and they didn't know how to get back. They were able to make it to the beach where we'd found them before the boat completely gave out, and they've been stranded there ever since.

"You guys didn't bump into anyone else while you were out there?" I asked, hoping not to get another earful.

"No, why? Did Dexter come looking for me?" Megan asked, looking genuinely concerned.

Her question through me for a loop and I didn't have the heart to tell them about Olivia, so I decided to be vague and let one of the adults be the bearer of bad news. "Some people came out looking for you, that's all."

"We can show you guys the way back to camp." Rodney added. "Unless you'd like to sleep out here, that is."

Megan shook the concern from her face and groaned while Diego thanked him before we switched our flashlights on and started back the way we'd come. We'd only made it to the base of the hill we'd come down when Megan noticed something floating toward us in the water. I could barely make it out until I had my light on it, and when I did, my stomach twisted. It was the bright yellow kayak I saw before, and it looked like something had chewed it up and spit it out.

Needle Like Teeth

"Holy shit." I muttered. "That's the kayak I saw on the island."

"It looks like a bear used it as a chew toy." Megan chuckled.

"You're sure it's the same one?" Rodney asked while he beamed his flashlight across it's

"It has to be."

"Just cause it's yellow?"

Barry waded into the water and started to pull it ashore. "I doubt they paint a lot of these things piss yellow."

"Fair enough." Rodney agreed before helping him get it up on the beach.

Megan hit the nail on the head when she said it looked like a bear had gotten to it. I couldn't tell if it was tore up by bite marks, claw marks, or something else, but it had enough holes in it that I was surprised it could still float. More concerning, though, was the thought of what happened to whoever had been piloting it.

I didn't get to ponder the question long, though, because the ringing got worse.

"Diego, it's happening again." Megan moaned while covering her ears. "I thought you said it was going to stop eventually."

"I know, baby. I'm sorry." He rubbed his own temples. "You guys are hearing that too, right? The ringing?"

"It's more of a buzz." Barry said, shining his flashlight over the water. "Not that it matters."

"We've heard it for a while now." I could feel a headache coming on. "But it's definitely getting worse."

"That means it's getting close." Barry turned his attention to the hill. "We should hurry."

Diego scoffed. "You really think some oversized lizard is out here controlling the weather, huh?"

As if to make Barry's point for him, a strong breeze kicked up and a thunderclap erupted in the distance. "See?" Barry grinned.

The noise in our heads had gotten to the point that all of us were either covering our ears, rubbing our foreheads, or scrunching our faces in defiance of the pain. Personally, I was just trying to ignore it, hoping to not repeat the crippling pain we'd felt the first time we encountered the sound. To be honest, though, there was a part of me that wondered how much of it was psychosomatic and how much of it was real.

Megan was lagging behind the rest of us, covering her ears as she went, when she stopped where the hill met the beach and stared down at something in the shallows. "Woah. What is that?"

The four of us must have turned in unison to see what she was seeing, because we all erupted into our own version of frantic warnings to get away from the water. Megan was looking at those two menacing green orbs, the eyes of that thing that almost claimed me and that, for all I knew, killed Olivia. She didn't listen, or maybe she didn't have time to process; either way, it was almost too late.

A crack of lighting landed somewhere behind us on the beach, and my mind tried to slow down time. I watched as the mysterious eyes pounced out of the water at Megan and saw its whole being illuminated in the bright, unforgiving light of the storm that had opened above us. It had the head of a salamander, a short bone-white horn poked out of its snout, its skin was black with markings of orange and red, its green eyes glowed duller above the water, and in total, I guess it was maybe twelve feet long from head to tail. The thing landed right in front of Megan; its head was a few inches taller than her waist, and when it let out a wet growl, I could see rows of needle-like teeth inside its mouth.

Megan let out a scream as soon as it leaped from the water, and Diego dashed down the hill toward her. Barry screamed for him to stop. Rodney yelled for everyone to run. Diego begged for Megan to back up. I froze again, speechless, and watched helplessly from the halfway up the hill. In the end, Diego pushed her out of the way right as the creature lunged and landed himself in its path instead of Megan.

Its jaws snapped so quickly that it caught Diego mid-air and locked it's jaw while the sound of crunching bones and erupting flesh filled the air almost as loud as our screams. The thing slid back into the water, dragging Diego with it. He wailed in pain at first, but everything happened so fast that I'm not sure he even had a chance to speak his last words.

I could see his blood polluting the water where he was, illuminated by the green glow of the creature's eyes. He was gone, but all I could think of was not dying myself. My throat stung from how loudly I yelled, "We need to go! Now! Right fucking now!"

Rodney and Barry helped Megan up the hill while I scrambled ahead of them like a coward. In my defense, I did wait for them to join me at the top before heading back on the path we'd taken before. The storm that had rolled in was in a full-blown rage by that point, with thunder that seemed to roar out one after another and lighting strikes beaming down so brightly and often that the dark of night was almost burned away. And the ringing, the buzzing, and the searing noise in our heads were only getting more powerful.

We'd made it to the same spot we first saw those eyes, with the drop-off on one side of us, when I fell to my knees from the pain. "Barry?" I yelled over the noise. "How do we make it stop?"

"I don't know!" He yelled back as he took a knee next to me. "I got an idea, though."

Rodney and Megan toppled over too, each of them covering their ears and howling in pain.

Barry pulled out a pocket knife, grabbed the back of my shirt, and cut off a section. He moved his lantern closer, cut a chunk of fabric into thin sections, and rolled the sections into small makeshift earplugs. I watched him put two of them into his ears and saw the relief wash over his face.

He handed me two more cloth plugs and barked above the noise, "Here," Before moving over to Megan and Rodney.

I did just as Barry did, and the sound was gone. My head still throbbed, and I could still hear the winds as they whipped through the woods and against my skin, but that terrible, crippling buzzing was gone, or at least dulled. It took me a moment to get a grip on myself and get to my feet, and when I did, I saw Barry fighting a losing battle.

He was trying to help Rodney, who was on the ground in the fetal position and refusing to uncover his ears. Then there was Megan, who'd gotten to her feet again but was swinging her body side to side as she stumbled with no sense of direction right next to the drop-off. My voice sounded muffled in my head when I called her name, and I got no response from her. She was only a foot or two from the ledge, so I dashed to where she was and grabbed her arm. Her eyes shot open as she yanked away from me.

Megan looked like she had tripped over something—a root or branch (not that it matters)—before she fell backwards. Her body flew off the edge into the open air below us, terror and confusion plastered on her face as she plummeted to the raging whitecaps of the lake. I don't remember if I called after her; if I tried to reach for some part of her to grasp too, I just remember the eyes.

Not her eyes, but those terrible green eyes that laid in wait below us. As Megan's helpless body hurtled toward the water, those emerald orbs seemed to grow brighter and closer. She didn't even hit the water, instead being intercepted by the jaws and needle teeth of the lake monster before dragging her under.

My mind couldn't bear to look at what happened next; instead, I turned back to Barry, who looked back at me, stunned and as white as a ghost. I shook my head back and forth as I felt resistant tears roll down my cheeks in droves. He motioned me over to him, and I could see Rodney was still fighting to let Barry help him. Something came over me; maybe it was good intention, maybe it wasn't, but I marched over to him and kicked Rodney in the stomach hard enough to get him to gasp for air and move his hands from his ears.

Barry scrambled to stuff the cloth in his ears, and we waited for him to catch his breath.

When he did, he looked at us and said, "Thank you." His voice was muffled through the plugs, but I could make it out. He asked, "Where's Megan?"

"She didn't make it." Barry answered calmer than I would have. He helped Rodney to his feet. "We've got to get moving, okay?"

"Yeah, okay." Rodney put a hand on his stomach where I'd kicked him. "Let's go."

Rodney and I had abandoned our flashlights, but Barry kept his electric lantern, so he led the way as we jogged back toward camp. The thunder and lighting had slowed, but the storm itself was still thrashing aggressively. Rain started to come down hard, and the winds kept wiping hard enough to cause leaves and pine needles to blow up from the forest floor and hit us in the face from time to time. It was bad enough that I debated if we should've just hunkered down somewhere in the woods, so when I saw a flicker of light I thought we were saved. There was a single, steady light in the dark of the trees north of the path.

I grabbed Barry's shoulder, almost causing him to slip and land in the mud. "You see that?" I asked, yelling over the earplugs.

He and Rodney both looked at the light. "Yeah, you think it's a place to dry out?" Barry hollered.

"What else could it be?"

"Good point." Barry shrugged, raised his lantern, and led the way.

About 60 feet from the path, we saw a small cabin. Well, it looked more like a shed than a cabin, with an aging porch and a single window. Inside, something was glowing bright enough to illuminate the whole interior space. Barry shined his lantern up and down the thing but didn't step any closer.

"What's wrong?" I asked.

"Someone's in there." He answered, not taking his eyes off the window.

"So?" Rodney asked. "Anything beats being out here in the rain."

"Rodney's right." I stepped onto the deck and put a hand on the handle. "If you want to stay out here, that's fine."

The inside couldn't have been larger than ten feet by eight feet, with a wooden bench against one wall, a few coat hooks by the door, a wooden stove warming the space in the corner, a single bookshelf filled with aging books, and a cot under the small window. Stepping inside, I noticed muddy tracks that led from the door around the cot. Rodney came in behind me and nodded toward them. I nodded back, took another few steps, and saw something that made my heart race.

Levi was sitting on the floor, breathing heavily, with one of his wrists handcuffed to a u-bolt that was mounted to the wall. He was covered in mud, and a small steam of blood ran from his forehead. Rodney and I looked at each other, stunned, before he went to his side and tried to wake him.

"Mr. White." He shook Levi, causing him to groan. "Mr. White, are you okay? What happened?"

"Rodney?" He wheezed.

"Yeah, it's me. What happened here?"

"You boys, you boys, you..." Levi started coughing and wheezing.

"Hey, hey, just slow down. Can you tell me who did this to you?"

Levi didn't look like he was in shape to answer.

"Barry's got that cellphone. I'll ask him if he's got a signal so we can call for help." I said.

"Good idea. I'll stay here with Levi."

I turned and opened the door with Barry's name on the tip of my tongue when I saw a flash of light break out of the shadows, followed by the crack of gunfire.

On Death's Door

"Holy shit!" I don't think I'd ever scream so loud. "Holy fucking shit!"

Barry's silhouette was highlighted by his lantern, and in that dim light, I could only see the outlines of his expression. It was shock—maybe a bit of fear—but shock through and through. His eyes fixed on something in the distance, but I couldn't see recognition in them, just wide pupils taking in one last still shot of the world before leaving it. Then he collapsed.

My instinct was to run to him, even though I knew it was a bad idea. That part of our minds that tells us it's normal and expected to save a stranger from a burning building kicked in. I scrambled to him, almost slipping on the slick collection of old leaves and pine needles that made up the forest floor. He was heavier than I expected; it took all of my strength to pull him by his arms the few feet to the cabin door.

When I managed to drag him inside, Rodney's eyes were wide in horror. "What happened, Eddie?" His voice shook.

I rolled Barry in front of the wood stove, then grabbed a pillow from the cot and stuffed it into the small window opening of the cabin. "I think someone shot him." I answered between labored breaths.

"Shot him?"

I nodded before getting on my knees and looking Barry over. There was blood racing out of a hole in his chest. My school required everyone to take first aid, so I knew I needed to put pressure on the wound. Using my hands, I pressed all my weight against it and tried not to squirm at the wet, warm feeling of Barry's blood trying to push through my fingers.

"What are you doing?" Rodney exclaimed, still frozen next to Levi's unconscious body.

"We've got to stop the bleeding. That's always the first thing you do."

"Is he still alive?"

It was a fair question, but one that my mind didn't want to consider. The idea of 'if' meant he could be dead, and I hadn't even processed the fact that I'd watched Diego and Megan get eaten by the thing in the lake. There's only so much the mind can take, but still, once Rodney brought it up, I couldn't ignore it.

I brought one blood soaked hand to Barry's neck and tried to feel for a pulse, but there was nothing. There was no sign of breathing, no pulse that I could find, and even his eyes looked dead. My friend was gone. Two of my friends were gone, and I was powerless to do anything about it.

We sat there in stunned silence for a moment, each of us seemingly absent of any idea of what to do next. I tried to run through my options, but none of them made much sense. It didn't matter if we ran, hunkered down, or made a stand; the truth of the situation was that someone was prowling outside and was armed. All we could do was hope and wait, but hope didn't seem to be in high supply.

Levi let out a wet cough, and suddenly my mind had a scapegoat for its frustration. He clearly was a victim of some sort of misfortune, but there was a chance he knew who had killed Barry. Even if it was irrational, even if it was a long shot, I was getting answers.

I marched a few steps over to his and slapped him with the back of my hand. "Wake up!"

Levi's eyes shot open, and his legs bucked in response. "What the hell?"

"Who did this?" I slapped him again for good measure.

He battered at me with his free hand. "What are you doing to me? Get off!"

I took my right heel and dug it into his thigh. "Answer me!"

Rodney jumped to his feet and pulled me back. "Calm down, Eddie. He didn't shoot Barry! Just calm down."

He mumbled a few well-deserved curses as he got his barrings. I waited for him to say something, to come to his senses, but he still seemed frazzled. Whoever had chained Levi up in that tiny shack had done a number on him. Dried blood and yellowed bruises covered his face and forearms, and his left eye was swollen.

"Well?" I barked. "Answer me!"

"I don't know what you mean, man. I'm just trying to sleep." Levi's words slurred as they slid from his lips.

I kneeled next to him, held his free arm down with one hand, and pulled his eye open with my other. His pupils were blown. "Fuck."

"What is it? What's wrong?" Rodney moved next to me.

"Look," I motioned to Levi, "his pupil isn't supposed to look that way. It means something's wrong with his brain."

"Like what?"

"Like a brain bleed, or his brain is swelling. Whatever it is, if he doesn't get to a hospital soon, he'll die."

We shared a panicked look with each other. For all we knew, someone was waiting outside to shoot us, or worse, was going to start firing into the walls at any minute. Barry's body was still leaking blood at a steady rate, and now Levi was on death's door. There was nothing we could do, or at least nothing we could think of.

"Well, we can't just leave him here." Rodney eventually broke the silence.

"We can't leave Barry here either."

"He's already dead."

"So?"

"So, we can't drag Levi's dying ass and Barry's dead ass through the woods in this storm." A clap of thunder broke out to add to Rodney's point.

"We've never seen this shack before. What if we can't find it again?"

"The cops have dogs for that, right? We'll just give them some of Barry's clothes for the scent, or something like that, and they'll find him."

I hated the idea of leaving Barry there, in the woods we barely knew, in a shack we'd never seen, to cool and decay as the wood stove he rested on slowly burned out, but Rodney was right. We'd lost Diego and Megan to the monster in the lake, we lost Barry to an unknown gunman, and we could lose Levi to whatever abuse he'd endured. It all felt like too much, and it was for how young we were, but we had a choice to make.

"Fine." I stood up and glanced around the room. "But we can't get him out of here until we get him out of those cuffs."

"I know a trick for that." Rodney pulled a multitool from his pocket and flipped it open to a set of pliers. "If these are like the older ones my dad showed me, I should be able to bend them here." He bent the latch and yanked it out of the catch, freeing Levi's wrist. "Just like that."

"When'd you learn that?"

Rodney shrugged and stood up. "I don't know, a while ago. I just never thought I'd need to do it in real life."

We didn't bother discussing what to do if we heard gunshots or ended up with a gun in our faces. I think we both knew in our own minds that we couldn't honestly account for something like that. Getting Levi to safety was our goal, and keeping that goal as our focus would help keep our nerves in check, hopefully. So we each picked up a side of him and shimmied our way out the small door back into the roaring darkness.

The storm was still raging; rain and wind were working together to make it feel like it was raining sideways, pelting us directly in the face. We worked our way toward Moonlight, hoping we'd find the trail we were on before, and as hard as it was, it did work. Even in the midst of that storm, we found our path, and by making sure the lake was on the correct side of us, we found our way back.

I didn't have any expectations for being met with a hero's welcome when we got back to camp, but I was shocked to be met with warnings being hurled by Sabrina.

"Put your hands up where I can see them!" She shouted, a gun drawn at us while rain rolled off her ranger's hat. "I won't ask twice."

We'd made it to camp, passed The Hole, and were just outside the Mess Hall when she stepped out into the storm and made her demands.

"Please, he's hurt and needs a hospital." Rodney pleaded as we struggled to keep Levi's limp body upright. "We found him in the woods."

"Put him down and back away." She barked through the rain at us, inching a half-step closer.

Levi must have been hovering somewhere between sleep, coma, and hypoxia because it felt like we were the only thing keeping his body from crumpling to the ground. The whole walk back to camp, his feet either drug behind him or tried and failed to take steps. He'd muttered a few things under his breath along the way too, but between the pelting rain and the sound of my blood pumping in my ears, I didn't catch what he'd said.

"We can't do that." I yelled back, trying to keep my voice from sounding agitated. "He needs a hospital. Can you get him to one?"

"Last warning." She took two full steps forward. "Let him go."

What calm I had left ran out there. "He needs a hospital!"

I look back on that day a lot, not just because of the pure chaos I endured but also because of how quickly people turned on each other. The day started with distrust around the money we'd found, continued with distrust between Levi and Downs, followed by Down and Murph, which led to us not trusting

Dexter and following him into the woods—and look what I got for it. Two people were eaten by some otherworldly thing in the water, and my friend was shot in the cold. Not to mention Olivia's apparent drowning.

"Ma'am," Rodney tried to calm the situation, "has something happened? Can you tell us why you need us to put him down?"

She twitched her weapon sparingly between the two of us, like she was deciding who was more likely to try something. It took a moment, but she landed on me and said, "Someone called in a tip and said they said two figures were dragging a body across their land. We still have multiple campers and staff unaccounted for, and now you two show up with the missing Levi White, looking like someone did one over on him."

"And?" I didn't hide my annoyance.

"And I'd say that looks pretty damning."

"Who calls in a tip at this hour? We didn't even leave the woods, who's land would be have been on?"

"Who comes wandering out of the woods at this hour?" She looked smug, but only for a moment. "You care to explain yourselves?"

Rodney and I looked at each other, and I could see his face pleading for me to tell her the truth, but I didn't feel like I could. We were already being treated like suspects, and telling her that we'd seen two people get eaten and another one get shot didn't seem to help our case. But also, I had no good lie kicking around my head that would serve as even a half-assed cover-up. The way I saw it, there was only one logical option: stall.

"Help him first, then we'll answer everything."

She took another step forward. "Give me a reason to trust you."

"Hey!" Rodney barked out. "He's not breathing."

I put my free hand on Levi's chest—nothing.

I'm All Ears, Eddie

I'd be a liar if I told you that I remembered what happened next; the truth is, I can only recall pieces of it. Like when you have a memory of a dream, it's there and your mind experiences it, but everything is dull and colored in pastels. I'm sure it was my psychology's reason for protecting itself; I'd already seen so much that night, and watching Levi's life circle the drain might have just been too much.

I remember Sabrina leading us into the Mess Hall and having us put Levi on a table, and I can recall the sound of Mrs. Leaver and Nurse Linda hollering at each other as they started to hover around him. At some point, Sabrina marched us back into the storm outside and brought us to the office cabin. After that, she must have cuffed Rodney and me together and left us there, because my memory only comes back into view when I was woken up by a stiff slap to the back of my head.

"Wake up." Sabrina demanded as she sat in Downs chair.

Rodney and I were handcuffed together and sitting in the same chairs that Dexter and I had found ourselves in on the first day of camp. Light was emitting through the aging blinds of the cabin, and I could hear the sound of calm, steady rain bouncing off the cabin's roof. Looking over at Rodney, I could see he was working on being awake, and I saw how filthy he was. It made me think about Barry and the blood I'd gotten on me, and sure enough, even after hiking back to camp in a thunderstorm, there were blood stains on my clothes, in the creases of my hands, and under my fingernails. If there was a poster child for guilty, I was it.

"Alright, talk." Sabrina put her mud-soaked boots on the desk and took a sip out of a chipped mug.

"Mornin' to you too, sunshine." I hissed as I rubbed the back of my head.

Sabrina shook her head. "No, nope, not happening, bud. You don't talk. I only want to hear from him." She pointed at Rodney.

Rodney's sleepy eyes shut wide. "What? Why?"

"Because this one," she said, shifting her bloodshot eyes to me, "keeps pissing me off, and I'm tired of his voice. So you get to be on the hot seat."

Rodney sat up in his seat and rubbed his forehead. "Okay. Have we been charged with a crime?"

"Hey!" She slammed the mug onto the desk, pulled her feet down, and leaned forward. "I said, I'm asking you questions, not the other way around."

"I'd be more willing to answer your questions if I was out of these cuffs." Rodney turned his Boston accent up to eleven. Something I'd seen him do before, but only when he was trying to show someone up.

Sabrina looked at him puzzled. "Excuse me?"

"Have we been charged for a crime?"

"No." She sat back in her chair, still wearing a puzzled face. "I just have some questions."

"Okay then. I'm sure, as an officer of the law, you know you can only legally detain us for so long without charging us for a crime, and that we are not required to answer any questions during that time." His eyes beamed into hers, like he was daring her to read his mind. "So we can either waste that time or make the most of it."

"Well, ain't you a bright one? Your accent, where's it from?"

"Lawyer."

Her puzzled look morphed into annoyance. "Oh, come on. Don't be a dick now, kid." Rodney shrugged, and she looked at me. "Are you in on this too?"

"Lawyer." I didn't see any reason not to trust Rodney's lead.

"For fuck's sake." Sabrina stood up, ripped her hat off, and threw it on the table. "I've got four missing campers now, a drowned counselor, and now the maintenance man is hanging on by a thread in the Mess Hall. Do you boys understand how royally fucked you are if I don't get some answers?"

"Lawyer." Rodney squawked.

Before she had a chance to scream any more questions at us, we heard the cabin door open and slam shut. Both of us tried to crane our necks to see who it was, and we managed to bonk our heads together in the process. Which caused a firm voice to snicker.

"Smooth." Murph chuckled. "You two ain't on the synchronized swim team, I take it?"

"What took you so long?" Sabrina barked before falling back into her chair.

Murph crossed the cabin, walked by me without as much as a glance, and parked his scrawny ass on the desk. "Sorry, Ranger Griner. The roads are still washed out. I had to take the onld farm road to make it back down here."

"Seriously? How long until the county sends someone out to make them drivable again?"

"A while, I'd guess. Last I heard, they were still dealing with flooding on the highways and a few compromised bridges. I even heard something about the old damn being at risk."

"Just add it to the pile." Sabrina turned her chair so her back was toward us. "You want to take a crack at these two?"

Finally, Murph acknowledged us. "Good to see you again, Eddie." He flashed a yellow smile from under his mustache. "Who's your friend?"

"Lawyer," Rodney said, making sure to highlight the Boston accent again.

"Nice to meet you, Lawyer. I'm Ranger Murphy, but you can call me Murph." He slapped his knee and laughed at his joke.

"Jesus Christ, you are lame." Sabrina groaned, still with her back to us.

By no means did I think I knew Murph well, but after everything that happened on the island and during his standoff with Downs, I felt I knew him enough to trust that he wasn't going to try to pin my friend's murder on me.

"His name's Rodney." I raised our cuffed wrists and shook them. "Any chance we can get out of these?"

Murph jumped from the table with his mouth ajar. "What on earth are you doing in those? Yes, yes, yes—here."

He fiddled with his keys and freed us. Even after nearly drowning, being shot at, getting attacked by a monster, and feeling Barry's blood rush between his fingers, I found the stinging pain that handcuffs left extremely unsettling. It was like the rush of blood going back into the space that had been squeezed so tight, which caused the pain. Being released from bondage hurts.

"Ranger Griner, do you care to explain yourself? These young men are not suspects, especially Eddie Matthews here. You know how helpful he was with that deranged camp director." He put his hands on his hips, just like I'd seen him do with Downs.

Sabrina turned her chair back to us and slouched farther down into it. "I know, I know, I'm just out of leads. Did you get the update about the missing campers and the maintenance guy?"

"Yes. Dexter, Diego, Megan, and Barry are all missing, and Levi White was recovered but in unstable condition. Right?"

"Yeah, that's right. But I'm telling you, Murph, there's something about all this that doesn't sit right."

"I hear you. I've never seen a grown man become violent over the threat of some make-believe monster, and as soon as he snaps his gourd, all these kids go missing, and that one girl, Olivia, comes up dead. It ain't right."

"That's what I'm saying!" Sabrina jumped up, snatched her hat from the desk, and threw it on. "I'm telling you it's got something to do with those robberies that happened a few years ago."

"You can't be serious."

"Come on, Murph, you've heard the rumors. A couple of drug mules went rouge, robbed some joints for the hell of it, and hid their drugs and cash in the old outlaw camp. It makes sense." Her eyes were wide with what I assumed was mania. "If we find that hideout, I bet we find those kids."

"Alright, let's say that the stories are real and that we can find them; how does that lead us to the missing campers and explain the assault that Mr. White endured?" Murph stayed glued to his power pose.

"I bet that one of them stumbled across it and found some of the cash, told the others, and got themselves stranded out there. Then, when Levi and Olivia went out looking for them, they came across someone else who was looking for the old hideout and crossed the wrong guy, or gal, whatever. It's a long shot, I know, but it's the only theory that fits."

"What about the timelines for the missing kids? Dexter and Barry went missing long after the others, right?"

"That's right." Sabrina leveled her gaze on Rodney and me. "And from what I understand, these two were with them, and only they came back."

"Oh really?" Murph turned to me too. "Care to explain?"

Rodney and I shared a look that said, 'We are so fucked' before he spoke in the calmest voice he could muster. "Give us the room, and we'll consider talking without a lawyer,".

They agreed and made sure to make a point of speaking loudly outside the door after they did leave, so we knew they were still there. Once we were alone, we weighed our options in whispers and tried to get our stories straight about what exactly happened. It turned out that we each had different views of that night.

"I didn't see her fall in." Rodney said while raising an eyebrow. "I just remember the buzzing, or ringing, or whatever the goddamn sound was."

"But you remember seeing that thing pull Diego in, right?"

He looked at the floor, trying to wrest the memory away. "Yeah, I do."

"Well, the same thing got Megan. I saw it myself. Barry did too."

"Barry did?" He looked back up at me.

The image of Barry's body in front of that wood stove flashed into my mind and made me shudder. "He did. I swear it, Rodney. You've got to believe me."

An unsettled look washed over Rodney's face, and he focused a hard stare on me. "You know what, Eddie? I didn't see Barry get shot either."

"What are you talking about? You saw him and you saw what happened to him. Hell, Rodney, you saw me try to save him." I didn't know I could get so pissed so fast. My mind begged me to deck him, but I only gritted my teeth.

"I heard the shot, and I saw the aftermath, sure. But I didn't see it happen. And I'm pretty sure you didn't bother looking for his phone either, which is what you were going to ask him about, right?"

"Rodney, where the fuck would I have gotten a gun?" I forced the words through my teeth without loosening my jaw.

"Whatever happened to that gun you snatched away from Downs? The one in the drawstring bag you were telling me about?" Rodney stood up from his chair and glared down at me. "It seems like the perfect time to swipe a weapon—in the heat of the situation."

"I tossed the bag to Linda." My blood was starting to boil

"That's what you're telling me, but again, I didn't see that happen."

I stood, looked up at him, and dug a finger into his chest. "You think I killed Barry?"

He shrugged, stood up and took a half-step back. "The only thing that doesn't make sense to me is how that lake thing works into this. I don't get it, and I'm not saying you did anything, but something ain't right here, Eddie."

"Why would I kill Barry?" I tried to ask without seeming angry, to keep tensions low, but I could feel how twisted my face was. I must have looked insane.

"Weren't you the one who pointed out that cabin too, where we found Levi?" He took two full steps back, working his way to the cabin door. "Just be honest, and I'm sure we'll figure something out."

I could read his mind. It was saying turn on Eddie, and make him the scapegoat. It'd be easy. "Rodney, please listen to me."

"I'm all ears, Eddie. They will be too." He turned to the door and hollered. "I'm ready to talk, and I think I've got bad news."

Lover's Lagoon

Rodney told them everything—sung like a canary is what my grandma would've called it—and didn't give me the decency of sparing any details. He painted a picture for the two Rangers that was so convincing that even God himself could have been talked into believing him. I don't know why I thought it, but part of me believed that we were better friends than that.

"So Diego and Megan were eaten by, uh, something, and Barry was shot and is dead in some unmarked cabin?" Sabrina asked with her eyes clenched shut, like she was trying to force the facts into her head.

"Yes ma'am." Rodney answered, sounding as calm as could be.

"And he saw all of it," Murph pointed to me, "and you didn't?"

"Correct."

"Huh." Murph leaned against the wall.

We had resumed our sudo interrogation in the same place, with the Rangers behind Downs' desk and Rodney and me sitting in the chairs we were originally cuffed at. Rodney had stepped outside to talk with them before they all came back inside. I was told that they weren't going to handcuff me to the chair or anything, but I still felt like I was unable to move, like any sign of resistance from me would be viewed as a sign of aggression, so I sat like my ass was glued down.

"What do you mean, huh?" Sabrina sneered at Murph. "We just got ourselves a witness to a murder."

"Well, technically speaking, we don't. Rodney said he saw Barry after he died, that Eddie told him Megan fell, and that Diego was eaten by whatever me and Lester were hunting down yesterday. So no, Rodney is not a witness to murder, he's just accusing Eddie of murder." He said it so matter-of-factly that it made my heart race.

"Wait, wait, wait." Rodney's calm demeanor started to sputter. "I'm not saying Eddie killed anyone. I'm just saying that he might have."

"Those are the same things, son." Murph answered while rubbing his forehead. "Do you have anything to add, Mr. Matthews?"

I felt like my freedom was being dangled in front of me, and at the same time, I was being continually reminded of the deaths of my friends. Looking back on that moment, I wish I could have responded differently—maybe take an extra moment to think through my emotions or ask for a lawyer one more time. Sitting there in the office, surely sleep-deprived and struggling to tread the waters of freshly planted mental trauma, I decided to give them a reason to suspect Rodney.

"We found a building on the island. Inside of it, there was a cashbox with a few grand in it. Everyone took a cut, even Levi. Maybe Rodney and Dexter decided to work together to keep it for themselves." I laid down my accusation with the composure of a seasoned poker player.

The Rangers gave each other a knowing look, and Sabrina asked, "What else did you find?"

I told them everything, from the night Dexter took us to the clearing where we first spotted the island up to the day I buried the cashbox and had my first up-close encounter with the monster that nestled out there. Sabrina was jotting down notes as quickly as she could in a small notebook she kept in her shirt pocket, and Murph kept leaning against the wall, nodding along as I spoke. Rodney began to slump into his seat the deeper I got into it, but he never dared to interrupt me.

Once I'd finished, Sabrina closed her notebook and looked at Murph. "If we can hunt down that box, we might find those kids."

"Or at least some clues as to where they ran off too."

Sabrina stared off into space for a moment, chewing on her cheek, then added, "We don't have a boat big enough for a rescue, though. The camp boat disappeared, and roads too washed out to haul in a new one. Kayaks and canoes won't cut it."

"I bet Mrs. Leaver knows where one is." Murph pushed off the wall and headed for the door. "Look alive, gentlemen, we're putting you to work."

Rodney sat back up in his chair. "I'd rather wait here, sir."

Murph pulled the door open, put one foot outside, and looked back. "You're welcome to wait in the back of my truck if you'd like. I'll even crack the windows for you."

Rodney stood up in a hurry. "No, that's alright. Lead the way."

Murph led the way, with Rodney and me behind him and Sabrina behind me, likely making sure neither of us tried to run off. As soon as we were outside, we could hear the rumblings of something in the mess hall. The sound of pissed off teenagers was emanating from within the building's walls, and it sounded serious. Both Rangers agreed they should check it out, just in case someone else had disappeared and Mrs. Leaver hadn't looped them in yet.

We followed Murph through the steel double doors of the Mess Hall and were met with a scene that looked like it was on the verge of a riot. Every camper was in there, all hollering over each other while Mrs. Leaver stood on a table, trying to corral the chaos to no avail. I didn't see Nurse Linda anywhere, so it looked like Mrs. Leaver was flying solo and failing.

Sabrina and Murph exchanged glances, then Sabrina took one step back out the door, unclipped her gun, and fired two shots into the air—the room fell dead silent.

"That's better." She said this before returning her gun to its place and stepping back inside.

"You boys take a seat, but don't get any ideas about taking off." Murph pointed to a table, where Kaya Smit was sitting by herself.

We took a seat, and the two Rangers joined Mrs. Leaver at the head of the crowd. Kaya seemed shocked to see us, probably because we were still coated in filth from the night before, but none of us spoke for a few minutes while Sabrina and Murph took charge of the makeshift assembly. The gist of what was happening was that every camper wanted to leave when news broke about Olivia's body being found and my friends going missing. But with the roads washed out and multiple telephone lines damaged in the storm, getting anyone out or even contacting families was difficult. As the Ranger relayed the message in a more forceful manner than Mrs. Leaver was able to, you could hear the frustration building in the room.

When they finally opened the floor for questions, Kaya moved a seat over closer to us and said, "I thought you guys were dead! No one's seen you since yesterday."

"It's a long story." I huffed. "Everyone here trying to bust out?"

"It seems that way, not that I blame them." She glanced across the crowd of campers.

"Them? You ain't itching to get home?"

Kaya looked back at us. "Not until I find Megan and Diego. With that storm blowing through last night, I'm worried that they'll get forgotten."

Rodney winced at the sound of their names. "Right. About that."

She cocked her head to the side, looking lost. "You guys found them?"

We told her everything. I'd like to say that I was compassionate enough to spare the details, but I didn't. I'm pretty sure that I was trauma-dumping just as much as I was looping her in. She just sat, emotionless and still, processing everything in stride.

As we talked, the mob in the mess hall started to become more and more agitated. I tried to tune it out the best I could, but I did catch pieces of the back and forth between Sabrina and the campers. It seemed that for every unsatisfactory answer she gave to someone's question, the crowd inched closer and closer to the ledge of a full-on riot. By the time we finished telling Kaya what had happened, the Mess Hall was full of scared kids who'd lost faith in the adults charged with their care.

"Can we get out of here?" Kaya asked, still seeming emotionally stiff. "I need to check something."

"I don't think so." Rodney said, moving closer to the table. "Ranger Murphy told us to wait here."

"I'll go with you." I said, standing up and offering a hand to Kaya. "They've got their hands full here."

Everyone in the Mess Hall was on their feet; some had even climbed onto their tables to shake fists or throw shoes. Anarchy was on the verge of taking control.

"What? You can't leave." Rodney looked at me with panicked eyes. "They said to wait here. You heard them, right?"

"Sure, I can. Besides, why would I wait around here? You'll probably just try to frame me for another murder anyway." Kaya took my hand, I helped her up and we pushed through the metal doors outside.

"Eddie!" Rodney hollered as the door closed behind me.

Kaya started jogging toward the girl's cabin, and I did my best to keep up. She led the way around the side of the lake I hadn't gotten to explore that year, which led into another chunk of woods that seemed basically untouched by people, with the exception of the overgrown path we were using. I kept looking behind me, half expecting Rodney or one of the Rangers to be hot on my trail, but no one ever came. In my mind, I knew leaving would only make me look more guilty, but I didn't let the thought linger.

We eventually reach a shoreline with a sliver of soft sand, hidden by willow thickets and ancient cedars. Kaya stopped, proped herself on her knees, and took a few deep breaths. "We're here."

I locked my hands behind my head and tried to catch my breath. "Where's here, exactly?"

"Megan called it 'Lover's Lagoon'. Apparently she found it last summer with some guy." She answered while scanning the area, looking for something to stand out.

"Diego?" I knew they'd met the summer before, but I didn't think they'd ever snuck off together.

"No. I think his name was Donald or Derek. All I remember about himwas that she said she gave him his head here and that his dick had a weird sideways curve to it." She snapped her fingers and pointed at a bush growing at the beach's edge. "That's got to be it."

I had a hundred questions about the mystery guy with a misshapen penis in his pants, but none of them felt like the kind of questions you want to ask a cute girl. "And what is it you're looking for?"

"If Megan's really is dead, like you say, then her family will want her stuff back. When she snuck off to meet up with Diego, she cleared out her bunk, and her duffel bag was gone. I'm hoping she brought it with her."

"You think the two of them were going to run off together or something?"

"Yeah, I guess so. It's the only thing I can think of that makes any sense."

Kaya marched over to the shrub and started digging around its sides and shoving her hands into its branches. I winced a bit at the thought of mindlessly scraping my skin against the drying, rough branches and imagined the sting she must have felt—she was determined. It didn't take long for her to pull out a small duffel bag that was so overpacked it looked like the only thing holding the zippers shut was willpower.

"Found it!" Kaya proclaimed as she trotted back to me. "You got anything against me opening it?"

It seemed like an odd question to ask, and given what I'd been through in the 48 hours leading up to that moment, it even felt trivial. "By all means." I motioned for her to open it.

She placed it on the ground, knelt next to it, and undid the zipper to the main pouch. Wadded-up clothes and zip-lock bags of makeup came oozing out of the duffel bag. Kaya began to sift through it all, making piles of clothes, hygiene products, and miscellaneous items. Then, at the very bottom of the bag, was a plain brown envelope. It wasn't sealed, so Kaya peaked inside and pulled out a single sheet of stationary paper with some Motel letterhead on it.

Kaya's eyes rushed across the page as she read, then she let out a gasp. "Holy shit."

"What?" I asked, pulling the letter from her hands. My eyes ran across it in the same rushed fashion that Kaya's did. It read:

Diego,

I'm so sorry you had to find out this way, but I didn't know how to break the news to you. I've had such an amazing time getting to know you through your letters and all those late nights on the phone, and being here with you these past few days has been incredible, but my heart belongs to someone else. One day, when you find real love like I have, you'll hopefully understand.

You have to realize that my parents won't accept my choices, and I need something to start my new life out on, so I'm taking the money for myself. I know you'd hoped to give us a good life, and I know one day you'll make someone happy—that someone just isn't me. Please don't try to follow me. By the time you wake up, I'll be long gone.

XOXO Megan

From A Breeze To A Roar

"Woah," was all I could manage to say, "she was really going to dump I'm through a letter?"

"Right?" Kaya took the letter back and started skimming it again. "Who do you think the other guys is?"

I shrugged, then knelt down next to the back and started sifting through the piles Kaya had made. "Maybe it's the dude with the sideways dick. Maybe it's some rando she met outside of here. Hard to say."

"True, still it feels off." Her eyes were bouncing from line to line, analyzing the letter for some clue or hint.

"Well yeah 'kid runs away from camp to start life a new with mystery man' it'd be a weird headline."

"Weirder than 'local camper eaten by lake monster'?" Kaya sighed. "I think that one would sell more."

I didn't disagree.

Kaya started digging through the make-up bags and I started going through Megan's clothes, checking the pockets of pants and looking for anything that could be hidden between the layers. I didn't expect to find anything, mostly because everything was wadded or balled up before it was stuffed in the bag, which made me think she did this in a hurry - that her sudden leaving wasn't pre-planned, but that didn't line up with the letter she'd wrote for Diego. Something rushed her plans along, but what? Then I felt something folded in the back pocket of a bedazzled pair of jeans.

I pulled out two folded up peices of paper, a map of Nebraska Sate Parks with yellow highlighter marked along highway 385 from Camp Alkali to the town of Ogallala and a bus route atlas with a highlighted path that ran from Ogallala, Nebraska to Salt Lake City, Utah. There was no writing on either, no encoded messages or half scrawled notes, just highlighted path - escape routes Megan planned to use on her way to a new life with her unnamed lover. Whatever she was up to had been plotted well in advance.

I handed them over to Kaya, told her what I thought, and gave her my theory. "So, what do you think?" I prodded after letting her examine the maps for a few minutes.

"Other then this makes Megan look like a basket case? I think we need to figure out what money she was talking about. There's no way she was going to be able to pay for this trip on her own." She looked up at me with suspicion in her eyes. "You got any ideas what she meant?"

I was used to that look in my everyday life. My mother would suspect me of something, ask me if I knew anything and stare me down with that same look. It was never clear if she was trying to be subtle or not, but either way, it made me quick to defense in every argument I had for the rest of my life. "What? Why you lookin' at me like that?"

"Seriously?" Kaya stood up in a huff and crossed her arms. "You're really going to play dumb?"

I stood to match her energy and was just tall enough that I could look down at her a tad. "If you asking, then you probably already know that answer. So, what are you getting at?"

Her face turned red with embarasement, even after being in the sun for a few days and the hardy jog to the beach, you could see her cheeks blush. She was caught. "Hey man, you're the one holding out on me."

"Fine." I turned, faced the woods we'd come through and started walking. "If you're going solo keep any eye out for danger."

"Eddie!" She squeeled. "Don't be an asshole."

That stung. I turned around and did my best to keep my face nuetral. "Then tell me what you know, then I'll tell you know what I know."

"You go first." She demanded, holding back swears and name calling.

"Not how this works."

Kaya chewed on her lip, frustrated that I wouldn't crack. "Fine, fucking fine. Diego told Megan about the cash you guys found on some island and she told the whole cabin about it. We all told her that he was just stringing her along, but she believed him. She only mentioned it a few times, but every time she did she'd space out, like she was seeing a ghost her something." Kaya turned her back to me and looked out over the water. "I'm just worried she went after it."

I walked toward her and planted my feet next to hers. The day was so calm that it felt out of place in the chaos of our human lives. Any other day, or under different circumstances, I would have said it was the perfect summer day.

"When we found her and Diego they were stranded on that strip of beach over there." I pointed to a sliver of sand at the base of the drop-off on the oppisite side of the lake. It was strange to look at it from a new angle, and I had to work to keep the image of Diego and Megan's death from my mind. "They were arguing, but we didn't get to the bottom of it before..." The word's trailed off.

"Before Diego got eaten?" Kaya scoffed.

"You don't believe me?"

Kaya shifted her feet in the sand and crossed her arms again. "I don't know. It sounds crazy, but so much of what's happened the last couple days has been weird."

"That's fair." In my mind's eyes I think I handled the situations I found myself in at Camp Alkali well, but in all honesty it was probably shock holding back waves of terror and grief. Kaya was right, everything had been weird, terribly unforgettable and sometimes unexplainable. Maybe her saying that is what made me trust her. "I buried the money, after we found it, by some trees on the island."

"Your joking, right?"

"No?" I squinted at her. "Why would I be joking?"

"You're telling me that on an island, that basically no one knows about, there's buried tresure? Like a pirate?"

She had a point, it did sounds like a joke. "To be fair, we only buried it to keep any one person from stealing all of it."

"We?"

"All of us who were staying in The Hole, even Levi. Everyone split it, except for me, I offered my split to Levi." My eyes fell on a rock that looked like a perfect skipping stone. I snatched it, flicked it toward the water and got three skips out of it. "All of them had something they needed the money for and I knew I'd have no way to sneak it by my folks so I passed."

"How much money was there?" Kaya asked, finding her own rock and managing to match my three skips.

"Six grand, give or take, it was all sitting in an old cashbox inside this shed on the island."

"You guys find anything else?"

"Not really. I did get attacked by something though, when I was burying it, there was some sort of animal den and I must have spooked whatever was there."

Kaya looked at me suspiciously again. "The monster that got Deigo and Megan?"

"I hope not," I let out a heavy sigh and let the weight of their deaths in, but only for a moment "but I think so."

We stayed there for a few mintutes, skipping rocks and looking out over the water. In all the unsettling things that I'd been apart of in the days leading up to that moment I'd started to think normal days were behind me, but in that moment I felt like an ordinary kid again, and it felt right. If I could have stayed on the beach with her for the rest of time, I would've - no questions asked.

"What do we do then?" Kaya asked, snapping me from my hopeful daydream

My shoulders sank and I took a deep breath. "Go show the letter to the Rangers. I'm sure they'll get it where it needs to go."

"I guess, but I don't know if I trust them, they're always so jumpy."

"Well, when we get back I'm sure they'll arrest me for something, so they might not even care about the letter."

"If Rodney keeps throwing you under the bus I bet you'll be behind bars in less than a day." She let out a laugh and punched my shoulder.

"Ha. Ha. Ha. That's super funny." I mocked.

"Oh lighten up. You'll be fine. Anyone with their head screwed on right can see your not a killer."

"Think so?"

"Know so." She flashed a smile. "Ready to turn yourself in, Outlaw Eddie?"

I put my hands in front of me, pretending to let her hand cuff me. "Make sure they know I came willingly." I laughed—it felt foreign, but good.

Before we had a chance to leave the beach, the wind picked up and the temperature dropped. A handful of clouds seemed to form out of thin air above the lake, and the still water I'd been admiring quickly turned to small, choppy waves. Kaya seemed to notice it, turning her attention to the water and catching a glimpse of something rolling across its surface.

"You see that?" She pointed to the lake.

Dancing with each punch of the tide was a wooden canoe, the kind that Camp Alkali used for all its activities, but that one looked like it'd been abused. I blocked the sun with one hand and squinted, trying to make out any details that I could. After a fair amount of staring, I could see the Camp logo and something slouched inside the canoe. It took a bit more focus, but then I recognized the shape—it was a person laying face down in their own lap with a jacket on and a hood pulled over their head.

"It's got to be Dexter, right? He's the only one still missing." The longer I stared at the bobbing canoe, the more concerned I felt. "But he's not moving, or at least, I don't think he is."

"Something about this is off."

"You think he needs help?"

Kaya walked to the edge of our little beach strip, waded a few feet into the willow thickets, and drug out a canoe that looked like the one on the water. "We can go after him in this."

"You knew that was here?" I asked before helping her push it into the water.

"Megan mentioned it. She told all of us where it was, in case we needed some alone time with a boy." As she said those words, I felt myself blush a bit and was sure to keep my head turned from her. "Anyways we..."

"We?" I cut her off. "No. You can't swim, remember? I got this."

She cursed under her breath. "I knew I shouldn't have told you that story."

"Keep an eye on me from here. If something goes sideways, go get help, okay?"

Kaya nodded and helped me get the canoe ready.

The canoe had a single wooden paddle inside that had been left in the sun for so long that it was more splinters than solid wood. Once we had the boat launched into the lake, I started pushing against the tide toward the drifting canoe. The current was pushing it in my direction, which helped, but the wind had gone from a breeze to a roar in the time it took to get out on the water, and that made it even harder to paddle. With each push against the wave, I felt a new sliver of wood dig into my hand, causing me to whiten my knuckle through the pain.

Kaya started yelling something from the beach, but between the waves and wind I couldn't hear her, all I could do was focus on my paddling instead. One stoke after another, that's how it works, even when it feels like it's not, just keep paddling. When I finally made it within a few feet of the wayward canoe, I could see whoever was in it had been strapped in and were bent over with their face in their lap. I yelled to get some reaction, but there was no response.

I'd hoped to pull the canoe back to shore with mine, but the waves had gotten too rough for that, so I'd only be able to pilot one. There was a moment of debate in my head between the ideas of trying to pull them into my canoe and trying to leap into theirs. Seeing that they were strapped in, moving over to his canoe made more sense. I lined the two canoes up next to each other and did my best to hold each steady as I stood to my feet to make the step over.

Each canoe wobbled with the waves, and I could feel them pulling apart from each other with each bounce of the tide. I'd managed to get one foot planted on each boat, so I pushed off from my canoe and felt all my weight start to sink on the other—I'd fucked up. In an instant I was in the water, had lost my paddle, and had filled my mouth with lake water. It would be dishonest to say I wasn't panicking.

I scrambled to keep my head above water and grabbed onto the canoe's sidecord with one hand. Once I was able to steady my breathing and calm my nerve, I noticed the boat pulling with the wind against the tide I felt at my feet. There wasn't much time left to get the stranded soul off the water before getting pulled deeper into the unknown parts of the lake. Finally, I managed to pull myself into the boat without flipping it.

"Dexter?" I barked between rough breathes. "You got to wake up man, there's a storm rolling in." I nudged his shoulder, but nothing happened. Being in the boat, close enough to examine the person in front of me, I noticed no moment in their back, and the skin on the back of their exposed hands had been sunburned to the point of blisters. A knot tightened in my stomach, I moved closer to them, and with one hand grabbed their hood and lifted their head up.

My eyes met with the dead, milky eyes of Lester Downs.

Ain't No Rest For The Wicked

Lester's skin had started to turn grey in the areas that hadn't been sunburned to all hell. His eyes were cloudy, almost milky looking, and his body had gone stiff with rigamortus - including his jaw with had clenched shut with his tongue hanging out. A deep red stain ran the length of his jacket, originating from a wound that a knife had been left in. It's handle was nothing fancy, cheap forest green plastic, same color Downs had the camp cabins painted in the off season, with no brand markings, seals or logos.

As soon as I registered that he was dead, and that I was holding him up by his hood, my mind and stomach went into shock at the same time. I dropped him back into his lap with a thud, and turned my head off the side of the boat worried I might vomit. After what I'd seen with Barry you'd think I would've been prepared for such a sight, but the truth is that death is ugly and not all of us are prepared to look it in the face without warning.

Once the sick feeling had passed and the racing thoughts of my paranoid mind had calmed, I looked to shore to see if I could flag down Kaya - but she wasn't there. The sliver of beach we'd been on, Lover's Lagoon as she called it, was no longer in sight. Either the wind had changed, or and undercurrent had taken hold of the boat, because I couldn't place where I was at all. I could see far off signs of land on both sides of me, but nothing close enough to make out. Lake Alkali was just wide enough that if an unfirmillar eye sat at the lake's center, it could fool them into thinking it was the ocean.

My eyes searched the horizon for a few moment, begging to find evidence that would prove there was no need to panic, but found nothing. I had no compass to point me home, no visible landmarks, and a dead body in the canoe with me. Weighing my options didn't make me feel much better, but there was some comfort in the idea that I was on a lake, so I could just paddle in one direction and I'd eventually find a shore. It was a good plan, until I realized there was no paddle in the canoe.

The panic I had barley managed to push aside came rushing back when I realized I was basically stranded. It's hard to say how long I spent spiraling, but it felt like quite some time. I yelled out for help, cursed the sun and waves, tried paddling with my hand, muttered curses and last rites to myself and even prayed. None of it made me feel better, and more importantly, none of it brought me closer to a solution. I decided that the mythical idea of fate had finally brought it's judgment on me.

The wind that I'd felt while trying to board Lester's canoe had calmed, and the boat floated aimlessly. I tried to make peace by taking a seat on the opposite side of the canoe from Lester, and stared into the sky. "Well, at least I won't die alone, right Lester?" I asked aloud.

"You could say that." A voice hissed.

I peeled my eyes of the sky above me and glued them onto Lester's corpse. "Hello?"

It was hard to say how much time had passed, and I was out under the unforgiving summer sun, but I'd thought I was pretty far from the point of heat stroke. To be fair my body and mind were already under a unfathomable amount of stress before discovering Lester, so maybe my mind snapped. Or it could have been lack of sleep, since I set foot on camp soil rest was rare and hearing things could be a consequence. Whatever the reason didn't matter, I heard a voice.

"You really should have seen your face, Eddie." It hissed again, a tad bolder.

"Excuse me?" I leaned forward and rubbed my eyes.

"At the beach fire, that monster story they told, you were on the edge of your seat and jumpy as hell. Like a dog in a thunderstorm." The voice took on a mocking tone.

"Holy fucking shit, I'm going nuts." I smacked myself across the face, praying I'd wake up from a bad dream or reset the circuitry in my head. "You're not real!"

"But I am, Eddie. I'm right here with you, baking away under the sun."

"No, no, no, no! I'm just tired, or deyahrated. You're just in my head. That's all."

"Only half true." The voice quieted.

"What's that mean?" The irratonal part of my mind was intrigued.

"I might be in your head, but he's in front of you."

"So?"

"So you'll eventually make it to dry land, and when you do those Ranger will find you. What do you think their going to say about you taking an afternoon canoe trip with Lester?"

"I'll tell them I found him like this. They'll find him eventually."

"*They won't believe you. Both of them already think you killed Barry and Megan, hell, by now Rodney's probably already changed his story and said you killed Diego too. Who's to say they wouldn't ship you off as soon as they found you?*"

"Fuck. That's a good point." The voice was making sense, which should have been a warning sign to me, but I was hooked.

"*Besides, maybe they don't have to find him.*"

"What do you mean?" I stared nervously, bopping my foot in place, causing the boat to shift from side to side.

"*Just drop Lester here in the lake. The scavengers will make quick work of him, and the lake is big enough that no one will come across him for a while.*"

"But they will find him. Then what? They could just blame me anyway. It's not like they're really looking for evidence."

"*True, but still, it'd look better if the body wasn't in the boat with you.*"

It was right; eventually I'd wash up on land, and it'd be a hell of a lot less incriminating if I was found by myself. I'd need to come up with a story about how I got there and hope that Kaya hadn't already told the Ranger what had happened, but I could cross those bridges when I came to it. Removing Lester was the only thing I could control, so that's what I did.

I pulled his body up by his jacket hood again and pulled the knife that was dug into his chest. There was a cracking sound as I pulled the blade out, followed by a hollow pop once it was free. The blade was caked in blood, so I rinsed it in the lake water and tried it on my t-shirt, leaving a streak of pink in its trail.

The blade was insanely sharp, and it made quick work of the strap that was holding Lester in. After he was free, I tried to straighten his body but couldn't; even his limbs and joints had become as stiff and resilient as an oak branch, so I had to accept the fact that he was going to a watery grave looking like a kid who fell asleep in their carseat. With a few good shoves, I got his body to the boat's edge and only needed to let go to send it into the lake.

"Well, Downs, I hope you find some rest." I said, releasing my grip and sending him splashing into the water.

"Ain't no rest for the wicked, Eddie." The voice said it, sounding like it was drifting away from me. *"That's what mother always says, doesn't she?"*

"How'd you know that?" No answers. "Hello?"

I peered over the edge of the canoe into the water and watched Lester's body drift into the dark. It looked peaceful, almost. Part of me wanted to dive in after him to look for some escape from my circumstances, but I knew better. There's no way of telling what was lurking down there, and my instinct was right. As Lester began to fade from view, a set of green orbs flickered to life in the darkness.

After how many times I encountered them, I no longer questioned what they were, and I didn't even look away. I watched those firmilar eyes rose closer to Lester, and then I watched as some unknown hand pulled him into the complete darkness of the deep water. The fact that I'd fed Lester's body to the Lake Alkali Monster didn't hit me until much, much later, but I've never really forgiven myself for it.

The voice must have sung with Lester because I never heard it again, even when I called out for it, begging to not leave me with my thoughts and my misery. The canoe had nothing useful in it to protect me from the sun, and all I'd thought to scavenge from Lester's corpse was the knife I pulled from his chest. I tucked in my belt, for safekeeping, and turned my attention to the blood stains that seemed to be splattered around the boat's interior at random.

I knew that being found after running off would already look bad, and being found after running off in a bloody canoe would be worse. Not as bad as being found with a body, but still damning enough to maybe warrant a night in the county jail. I tried scrubbing the dried blood with my hands and lake water to no avail, only managing to fill my hands with more splinters. The only solution I could think of was to make it look like it was my blood.

Weighing my options led me to a couple different stories. First, I could cut my wrists shallow enough to not kill myself but make it look like I tried. I could say I was distraught at the thought of being falsely blamed for Levi's death and decided to take matters into my own hands. Initially, I knew that would land me in mandatory therapy with either my parents or a judge, which wasn't something I was interested in. So my second option was to make a cut deep enough and jagged enough to look like an accident, which could have been caused by a million things. I went with the second one.

The story I decided on was to make it look like the knife I had found slipped and sliced between my left thumb and pointer finger. I'd actually done it to myself once before on a family fishing trip in the seventh grade, and I still had a noticeable scar to use as a blue print. My hand tiwitched as I brought the blade to my skin, and it took five deep breaths to calm my nerves. The knife cut into my skin with ease, and I did my best to follow the old scar, making sure it looked random, and then it was done.

As I pulled the blade away I felt the rush of hot, searing pain flood my hand. My voice let out a weary scream, but my heart wasn't in it. I felt woozy, my vision started to dance and I had a sudden feeling of peace in my chest. There wasn't even time for me to wrap my hand in anything before I passed out. That cut was the last straw, my mind and body gave out, and I don't blame them. There were no dreams, or fragmented moments of consciousness, only a large blank spot in my memory - until I was woken up, that is.

"Eddie." A voice called to me, causing me to flutter my eyes. "Eddie, wake the fuck up man."

"Huh?" Was all I managed. Every fiber of me hurt, and the simple action of muttering caused a twinge of pain in my throat.

"Eddie," They said, before slapping me across the face, "I said wake up!"

My eyes shut open and I scrambled to a sitting position. Kneeling in front of me was Dexter.

"Well, fuck, I was starting to like the idea of eating you." He grinned, stood up, and stuck out his hand. "So what happened to you anyway?"

The Future. My Future.

I was too stunned for words, too stunned for thought, and too tired for reason. For all I knew, I'd died and gone to some sick version of hell where I got stuck with Dexter in a boat, and that truly sounded like the worst kind of hell I could imagine. Everyone has a fight or flight instinct when faced with danger. I chose flight, fought my way to my feet, dove over the canoe side expecting water, and hit earth.

"Jesus Christ, Eddie!" Dexter exclaimed, stepping out of the boat and onto the beach I landed on. "Did you hit your head or something?"

I scrambled to my feet and spun a time or two, trying to get a sense of where I was. The sky was darkening, leaving only its trademark watercolor sky of purple and orange; a spattering of trees sat on my left, and the dark, cool tide of the lake sat on my right, and gleaning in the last rays of sunset in the distance behind Dexter's concerned look was a patch of tin roof. After a whole day floating without direction, I managed to land on the Lake Monster's island.

"What the fuck is happening?" I muttered half to myself.

"That's what I'm trying to figure out." Dexter said, stepping toward me and putting a hand on my shoulder. "How'd you end up all the way out here?"

I didn't answer him for a moment, choosing to collect my thoughts and ground my perspective first. "I could ask you the same thing. We saw you leave the cabin, hell, we even chased after you! What's going on, Dexter?"

He dropped his head and twisted his shoes in the sand for a minute. "It's going to be dark soon. Let's get inside where it's safe, and then we'll talk."

Dexter guided me from the beach, through the mess of shallow roots, and to the shed. Once he opened the door, though, it looked completely foreign. The entire space had been packed with supplies and cleaned up. There was a floor lamp from the mess hall hooked up to some sort of solar panel, a rug from a cabin, a blow-up mattress, stacks of canned food, and two bundles of bottle water.

"Come on in." Dexter motioned for me to step in ahead of him.

"Did you do all this?" I asked as I entered, trying to make sense of what I was seeing.

"Yeah, it took a few trips, but it turned out." He latched the door behind him, stepped past me, and grabbed a first-aid kit from inside a backpack that was on the mattress. "Let me see that hand."

"When did you have the time?"

"Well, I didn't have a lot." He answered as he began to clean the cut on my hand with alcohol swabs. "Pretty much any time I snuck off, I was working on it."

"But how'd you get all this over here? And where'd it come from?"

"Camp mostly. I just took what I figured I needed." He took out an oversized bandage and covered the wound. "Getting it out here was the hard part. I ended up using two kayaks at a time, one to get me across and one to carry whatever I was bringing."

"I'm surprised no one noticed two kayaks missing." I quipped while trying to ignore the stinging in my hand.

Dexter got up and put the kit away. "I found these two obnoxious yellow ones in that covered dock that Levi showed us. I guessed no one was paying attention to them. But something happened to one of them. I left one tied up on the bank after my last trip." He grabbed two water bottles, handed one to me, and sat on the floor with to me. "But it's gone now, so I guess someone did come looking for it.

The yellow kayak, the same one I saw with Downs and Murph, and the same one I saw shredded on that strip on the beach after finding Diego and Megan—it was Dexter's. It had to be; that was the only answer that made sense. But of course, the question was why he set up a makeshift home in the first place. I had an idea of how to find out.

"How'd you make it out here? The other night, I mean. It got nasty out in a hurry after you disappeared, and we lost you pretty quick."

"No shit. I thought a tornado or something was coming based on how bad that wind was howling." He got up, walked to one of the shelves, picked something up, and tossed it at me. It was a key tied to an orange length of paracord. "I used these."

"You took the camp boat? The one from the dock?" I was genuinely shocked, even though it made no sense to be. "Where is it now?"

He walked back over to me and sat back down. "It wasn't my first plan. I was going to use the yellow kayak, but the water was too rough. Besides, I knew I was going to need something quick when it was time to bounce for real." Dexter paused for a moment and chewed the inside of his cheek. "But that *thing* had other plans."

I didn't even have to ask; I knew what he was talking about—the monster that seemed to grow fond of toying with me and snacking on my friends—it took a stab at him. "What happened?"

Over our summers together, I had the displeasure of spending enough time with Dexter to learn his expression, and as he told me what happened, I could see he was being honest and reliving a horror. He told me about how he was already planning to ditch camp and how he had planned to only be on the island for a few days, hoping anyone who'd be looking for him would assume he had already left the state. Using the boat Levi had shown us, he cut across the waves in the dark, hoping to not draw attention to himself, until he finally came up on the island's shores. It was while he was looking for a place to drop anchor, as out of sight as he could be, that he noticed the eyes lurking in the shallows.

Dexter said his gut told him to scare it off, to show it he was bigger than it—the same way you do with a mountain lion. He grabbed one of the flare guns from the boat's main compartment, but when he went to fire it, the eyes were no longer there. Every fiber of him told him to run, but jumping in the water seemed worse than standing his ground, so he scrambled to each side of the boat looking for those ominous green orbs, but there was nothing—until he heard something crunch beneath him, followed by the sound of water filling empty space.

Hearing that sound put him in the back seat while his need for survival took the wheel. He dropped the flare, threw himself over the side, bellyflopped in water just deep enough to catch him, and hurried to shore. When he reached the small spattering of trees, he looked back to see the boat sinking and a huge, slick, black creature latching to its decending hull. The thing peered back at him and let out a low, wet growl, which sent Dexter sprinting for the shed.

It didn't chase him, and it hadn't bothered him since. He said he almost wondered if it was even real because the whole time he crossed the water, he heard ringing in his ears, and when he saw the monster, that same ringing got so bad, he felt like he could pass out. Maybe it was a trick of the mind, he said, like when little kids convince themselves there really is a devil under the bed and they won't dare look under it—even in daylight, even with good old mom and dad.

"You really haven't seen any sign of it?" I asked, pulling myself to my feet to stretch my legs. "It'd have to be massive."

Dexter got up, went over to the door, opened it just enough to peek out, and closed it again. "To be fair, I haven't really gone looking for it. But sometimes I think I hear it, and I just stand really still."

"With the boat gone, how'd you plan on getting off this rock?"

"I started building a raft, but I'm not sure how well it'd hold up. Now that you're here, though, I won't have that problem. Who knew Eddie Matthews would turn out to be a good luck charm, washing up in a perfectly good canoe?"

"Don't count your lucky stars yet." I scoffed. "It's got no paddle."

"Making a paddle has got to be easier than making a raft. I think we'll figure it out."

"Fair enough." I looked around the cabin, feeling my empty stomach making itself known. "Is there anything I could eat? I honestly don't remember the last time I had a meal."

He looked at me with nervous eyes, bordering on scared, and walked over to the pile of canned goods he'd stacked in one corner. "Well, uh, I kind of had a plan for all this." He folded his arms with his back to me and hung his head. "But I don't know anymore."

It clicked. "This was all for Megan, wasn't it?"

Dexter's shoulders stiffened. "What did you say?" The words were forced through clenched teeth.

"I found a letter she wrote Diego about how she was going to run off with someone else and how she was going to take the money. You're the mystery man, right? Her secret lover?" I tried to keep my tone level and to sound genuine.

He turned to me and dropped his arms to his side with balled-up fists. "Why hasn't she shown up yet?" His voice cracked. "Where is she?"

"Dexter, I think you should sit down."

He refused to sit and demanded that I give it to him straight. I tried to put things lightly and dance around the harshness of some of it all, but anytime I took a second to choose my words, he'd get more agitated and demand I stop treating him like a child. Despite my better judgment, I did just that and told him everything. From Diego and Megan, to Barry and the shack, to Rodney accusing me and running off with Kaya, all the way to the letter we found, dumping Downs into the lake and slicing my own hand. No detail was spared, no stone was left unturned, and the whole time he stood there frozen.

There was a long silence after I finished; neither of us moved, and the only sound was the night breezing brushing against the shack to remind us the world was still out there. Finally, he asked, "She's dead?"

I nodded, afraid that answering aloud might trigger something in him.

"You're sure?"

I nodded again.

"Who killed Barry then? And Downs?" He shook his head from side to side and squeezed his eyes shut. "It doesn't make any sense."

"I don't know, Dexter. I don't know."

"I can't believe Megan's gone." Tears began to rush down his face, and his breathing became choppy. "We were going to figure it all out, you know? She told me about all the places we could go."

"Dexter, I am so sorry." Were the only words I could think of to say.

He stomped across the room from me and wrapped me up in the most desperate bear hug known to man. "She was supposed to make it all better, man. She was the future. My future." A few uneven breaths and gasps escaped his chest. "She was going to save me, Eddie. She really was."

I placed my arms on his back; it felt foreign and wrong, but I'd seen that kind of pain before. It was the kind of pain that made decent people turn sour and innocent kids turn hateful. Dexter was feeling hope die. The same thing turned my own mother from a sweet caregiver to an annoyed jailer. I didn't want that for him—for anyone, honestly.

"We were going to be a family, Eddie. Me and her against them all." The words stopped, and the wails began.

Dexter went on to tell me about how they had a fling the summer before but kept in touch. It turned out Megan was courting a few guys at once, keeping her options open, so it seemed, but had a soft spot for Dexter. He opened up to her about his home life, the abuse he faced at the hands of his parents, the terrible things his uncle did to him when no one was around, and the unspeakable things his inner voice begged him to do. Megan took it all in stride and promised to fix him, to help him start anew, and most importantly, to put distance between him and his family. They didn't know how or when, but they'd figure it out. Then we found the cashbox.

He told me everything like I'd already known about it, like he was talking to an old friend, and in a way, I suppose I was. Even though I hated his guts, we'd gotten stuck with each other every summer since the fourth grade, and that meant we had history. We knew about each other's crushes, crazy siblings, surface-level fears, and what buttons to push. So we sat on the air mattress and ate beans from the can, talking about our fucked-up lives, how terrible the camp really was, and who could have killed Barry and Downs.

Dexter, even through his pain, had an idea. "You know what? I bet the killings have something to do with the cocaine."

I choked on a mouthful of baked beans. "What cocaine?"

He put a finger up, telling me to wait, got on his knees, and pulled up a section of the plywood floor. Underneath were multiple brown squares that looked like they'd been wrapped in packing tape. Dexter picked one up that had a cut in it and cracked it in half, sending white particles all over the room.

"See?" He said he waved the particles from his face. "It's cocaine."

Pile Of Bones

I wouldn't go as far as to say that I was a bad kid or that I was looking to get into bad things, but I had run into cocaine twice before. Once, when I was seven and asked to testify at my cousin's trial, he was charged with drug trafficking and also happened to serve as my emergency babysitter when my parents were out of options. Somehow, someone had learned that I had been at his place a few times and was asked if I'd seen a brown package covered in packing tape before, just like the ones Dexter had shown me - I had.

The second time was at a house party I'd snuck into with two of my friends. It was the night of high school graduation, and a bunch of seniors had decided to throw a rager in a dilapidated cabin outside of town to celebrate their new-found freedom. Me, my friends, and a handful of other brave underclassmen decided to crash the party and were met with forms of debauchery that we simply were not prepared for—not that it stopped us from indulging. I could say with confidence that cocaine was not for me.

"No fucking way." I exclaimed, rubbing the fine white powder between my fingers. "How much is there?"

Dexter shrugged, put the package back, and dropped the plywood floor into place. "I don't know, but it looks like a lot. My mom watches a lot of cop shows, and they always talk about drugs in grams. How big do you think a gram is?"

Under different circumstances, I would have welcomed ridiculing him for not knowing. "A gram is tiny, like really, really tiny."

"Oh." He scratched his chin and put one hand on his hip. "So there's a lot of grams here, then?"

"Yeah, probably fifty to a hundred pounds is what's here." I took a deep breath and sat back down on the air mattress. "Does anyone else know it's here?"

"I doubt it." Dexter said this while sitting down and riffling through his backpack. "But I did find this taped to one of the, uh, boxes?"

"Bricks." I corrected.

"Excuse me?"

"They're called them bricks of cocaine. At least that's what they call them in the news, like when they catch someone with them on TV, they say 'he had 3 bricks of cocaine' or something like that."

"Got it. Then I found this taped to one of the bricks."

He stretched his arm out and handed me a slip of paper. It was a strip of pink receipt paper, the kind you'd get from a mom-and-pop shop or the middle of a no-where fuel stop, folded in four. The color had faded from the edges, and the ink started to bleed in a few spots, likely from moisture trapped under the floor, but it was still mostly legible.

S.M,

When you find this, if you find it, I just want you to know we blame you. This whole plan was blown to hell from the jump because of you, and the boss isn't going to take kindly to it. If we had just done what we were told and moved it bit by bit to Colorado, things would have been fine. Staging robberies to throw the state patrol off only brought more heat, and now we've been waiting two days for you and you haven't shown up. All you had to do was pick us up and move the product, but you couldn't even manage that. If we're dead, we better be haunting you.

Fuck you,

L.D. and G.F.

"Huh." I folded the note and handed it back to Dexter. "Any signs of someone else being here before us? Other than the cash and the coke?"

"There's some old boat half buried on the beach and a grave on the other side of those trees."

"A grave?" I tried not to look suspicious, but the thought of a secret grave on that spec of dirt seemed unlikely.

"Well, I think it's a grave. There's just a hump in the ground with a cross made of sticks next to it."

After all the insane and unexplainable things I'd experienced so far that week, all I craved was an answer, a single answer to any one of my building questions, and one presented itself. Is there actually a grave on the island? One way to find out is to go dig it up.

"You got a flashlight I can borrow?" I asked while jumping up and grabbing a shovel from the pile of hand tools that had been sitting so long that a quarter inch of dust had formed on them.

"Sure." Dexter pulled something from his bag and tossed it to me. "Are you going out alone?"

"If I have to," I said, going to the door and pulling it open, "but you're welcome to help me."

He chewed on his cheek as he weighed his options. "I don't know Eddie. It's late, and I can't stop thinking about Megan being gone."

"I get that. Barry and Diego are gone too, and I'm pretty sure Levi's dead on a table in the Mess Hall now, but sitting around isn't going to change that." I opened the door the rest of the way and motioned outside. "So you coming or not?"

He didn't answer, but he did grab his own shovel and stepped outside. He was adamant about making sure the door was latched before showing me to the grave. The grave Dexter had found wasn't far from the shed, maybe 30 feet, just on the other side of the trees where I'd buried the cashbox and had my first up-close run-in with the creature that had eaten my friends. I was aware of where we were, but I was so determined to find one goddamn answer that I chose to ignore the sense of danger.

Dexter's description of the grave was spot on: a shallow mound on the beach, with two sticks tied together with shoelaces to make a cross. The sand that covered it looked worn and settled, so it couldn't have been fresh, and the shoelaces that held the makeshift grave marker together were completely unbleached. My hunch was that it had been there for a while, so hopefully we'd only find a skeleton once we got deep enough.

"You think we'll go to hell for doing this?" Dexter asked as I speared my shovel into the mound.

"Dexter, you mean to tell me, with the amount of trouble you find yourself in, that you believe in hell?" I began moving the earth.

He shrugged and dug his shovel in. "I guess I just hope there is."

"You hope there's a hell." There was no hiding my shock at the statement, but Dexter wasn't phased.

"Sure. I hope that at the end of it all, the real assholes get what's coming to them, you know?"

I didn't blame him, and I still don't, for looking at it all that way. All the terrible things he told me he endured would be enough to make anyone pray for righteous fire to come down. Even in my own life, in a much smaller way, I hoped that one day the people who put me down or made me feel small would get a taste of their own medicine. Was it a healthy outlook on life? No, probably not. But it was one that gave us hope, and hope is the fuel of the damned.

"I know what you mean."

We worked quietly for what felt like ages, moving sand and gravel and trying to keep it from sliding back into the grave as we got deeper. It was about four feet down when we heard our first 'thud' under the blade of the Dexter shovel. There was no coffin or cobbled-together box, though, one bone. Before long, we'd gathered enough bones to make a small pile next to where we dug. Neither of us could tell what was what, besides a skull and a jawbone. Even though we'd just unearthed human remains, I was frustrated because I wanted more answers.

"Jesus fucking Christ." I tossed my shovel out of the hole in frustration and dropped to my knees.

"Right?" Dexter said, pulling himself to the surface. "This is insane."

"But how do we tell who it is? There's got to be a way to, like, identify this dude." I started scratching through the dirt with my fingers.

"I don't know, Eddie. Maybe the cops can figure it out."

I was going to protest and tell him that the cops couldn't know about it and that I couldn't risk being killed by yet another dead body, but I didn't get the chance. Something slick and solid hit against my hand as I dug and pulled up a wallet. Partially decomposer leather, held together by plastic-lined stitching, and full of plastic cards.

"Bingo!" The word jumped out of me as I pulled myself up. "Hand me the flashlight."

Dexter held the light above me, and I began placing the cards on the ground. There were a handful of credit cards: an Omaha City Library card, a pocket-sized, water-damaged Polaroid, and a student ID card from Chadron State College. Every card had the same name as one of them: Garret Fowler.

"G.D., from the note?" Dexter asked, holding the student ID in his face.

"I'm willing to bet. It looks like the story Megan told us about the gas station robberies was true, huh?"

"Yeah, just not as straight-forward as she told it." He put the card back on the beach with the others. "Who do you think L.D. is?"

"No idea; there isn't another grave for us to check, is there?"

"What? No." Dexter put on his classic bully tone, signaling to me that we were getting too comfortable. "Who would have buried the other guy, genius?"

"Yeah, yeah, yeah. We're stuck together, so let's get along." I reminded him while putting the cards back into the wallet and placing them on the pile of bones.

Dexter let out a sigh and added, "Fair. But I do have a hunch, if you promise not to be a smart ass about it."

"Really?" I raised an eyebrow.

"Lester Downs." He opened his eyes wide, as if that made it more dramatic.

"Didn't she say they died out here last year? Downs is like 45; there's no way he's a drug mule."

"That's a fair point." He tapped his shoe in the sand nervously for a minute. "Should we put it back then? We could burry the bones, but keep the wallet and just say we saw it out here."

I nodded while thinking it over. It wasn't the perfect plan, but it was better than reporting another dad. "Yeah, good idea."

We'd both just picked up our shovels when we heard a low humming sound start to grow somewhere in the night. At first, I wondered if it was a cicada, getting louder and more pissed off in one of the trees, but then there was the light. A bright beam started bouncing across the water, powerful enough for me to know it was a spotlight. Either Murph and Sabrina had come looking for me or one of their friends.

"Fuck, fuck, fuck." I dropped to my hands and knees. "We need somewhere to hide, man. It's the rangers."

"Isn't that good? The can get us out of here."

I shushed Dexter and yanked him down to my level. "If they find us, they're going to pin me for murder and ship you back home; do you want that?"

Fear flooded his gaze, and even under the dim moonlight, I could see the color flush from his face. "Can't we just hide in the shed?"

"One of them already saw the shed before, and if Rodney's with them, then he'll show them where it's at. Is there anywhere else we can hide?"

Dexter looked at the ground for a minute, stringing his options together, and then said, "Follow me."

We crawled on our hands and knees to the spattering of trees and maneuvered over the minefield of roots. I could see the spotlight getting closer and hear the hum of the engine growing louder with each second, and my heart started beating faster and faster with each stride I took. The spot that Dexter had led me to was completely black, with the canopy of pine trees blocking out the moonlight.

"Trust me." He said this, flicking his light on and revealing a deep hole in the ground that sloped at an angle. "It's our only option," he explained before sliding down feet first.

The hole looked damp, and even in the dark, I knew where I was—the burrow where I saw the monster. Still, Dexter was right; I had no other options. I slid my feet in, closed my eyes, and pushed off into the darkness, hoping that no one was home.

June

There's a feeling that you get when you realize that you just did something incredibly stupid. Most people first feel it in early grade school when they decide to color outside the lines on purpose to get a reaction or when they figure out that pulling girls pigtails doesn't get them any closer to holding their hand. It's a mixture of embarrassment, disbelief, and shame, and that feeling hit me like a freight train sliding into that burrow after Dexter.

Between the two of us, we only had one flashlight, and Dexter had it. When I landed at the bottom, he shined the light on me, nearly blinding me in the process. "You good?"

"I'm fine." I grunted, dusting myself off and standing up. "Have you been down here before?"

"Nope, but I figured it was better than trying to climb a tree." Dexter cast the flashlight around the space, exposing its details.

I was surprised that the whole space hadn't caved in at some point. It was wide, about the length of a car, and tall enough for me to stand up straight. The walls were rough-edged raw dirt, and the floor was a mix of mud and half-dried lake scum. Looking around reminded me of the pictures I'd seen in the school book about beaver dams and salamander burrows.

"This is insane." Dexter said panning the light opposite of where we'd entered. "It looks like it keeps going too."

His light landed on what looked like a tunnel, where
the earth ceiling began to shorten.

"Oh, fuck that." I whispered, taking three steps backward.
"Nothing good can be in there."

"Seriously, Eddie?" Dexter flicked the light onto my face.
"What the fuck are you so afraid of?"

"Whatever made this place, obviously."

He waved, dismissing my concern. "It's probably just some
beavers or something."

I never considered him to be a bright kid, but that
comment deserved a follow-up question. "Dexter, how big do
you think a beaver is?"

He shrugged before turning the flashlight back to the
tunnel. "I don't know, the size of a goat or something like that."

"And you think an animal the size of a goat could do this?"

He waved his hand again. "For fucks sake. How big is a
beaver then, Mr. Know-It-All?"

All I could do was sigh and shake my head. "Honestly, it's
not important."

Before we could continue our debate about the size of
beavers or whether to go deeper into the burrow, a firm voice
barreled out above us.

"Eddie, if you're here, please respond." It was Sabrina's
voice, distorted by static, probably using a bullhorn. "Eddie
Matthews, are you out there?"

"Oh shit! You weren't lying, were you?" Dexter asked in a
half-whisper.

"Obviously." I hissed while my mind scrambled for possible
escape routes. "We need to move."

Dexter didn't miss a beat. "Guess we're going in the tunnel then, ain't we?"

I let out a frustrated groan and rubbed my temples. "Fine, but you lead the way. I'm not getting eaten because I was stupid enough to follow you."

"Hurtful, but fair." I could hear a smile in his voice; it worried me.

He led the way, just as I asked, into the tunnel that got tighter and tighter. After a few feet, we had to crouch to keep moving—not so low that we were on our knees, but enough that we had to be mindful not to hit our heads. The width of the tunnel was just as wide as the hole that reached the surface, which made me wonder more about what exactly could carve shapes like that into the ground.

We only had to travel about twelve feet before the tunnel opened into a wider space, about half the size of the main burrow but tall enough for us to stand up again. Dexter still held the flashlight and beamed it around the space just long enough for two things to draw my attention. The first was something dark and slick on the opposite side of the space that seemed to be half buried in the wall of dirt. Second, there were three curved objects along one of the walls.

"Hey, shine your light on that again." Dexter did, and the flashlight revealed three spotted eggs, about the size of soccer balls, resting in what looked like a nest of mud and debris. "Are those..."

Dexter didn't give me a chance to finish the thought. "Eggs? Yeah, pretty sure they are." I couldn't see his face behind the light, but I could still hear that smile on his voice.

"What is this, Dexter?" In an instant, I could feel my heart rate rise and my palms start to sweat. I'd seen enough bad things that week to know a bad omen when I saw it. "What's happening?"

"Like I said, they're eggs. Maybe beaver eggs, or maybe the eggs of whatever thing you said ate Megan." He sounded sinister and angry, but mostly desperate. "Hard to say for sure until one of them hatches or until the mom comes back."

"Beaver, don't lay eggs." I muttered while my brain went into overdrive, thinking of what to do next. Above ground, Sabriana was looking for me, probably with backup, and below ground, I was trapped with Dexter and monster eggs. A real rock and a hard place situation.

"I know that." He moved the light off the eggs and onto me, and there was just enough glow to reveal his face. His eyes were sunken, and his brow was furrowed—it made my skin crawl. "I found this place after Megan didn't show up. I wondered if it'd be useful at all."

"Useful?" I asked while trying to figure out the odds of overpowering Dexter without alerting the Ranger above us that we were down here.

"Sure. I figured they belonged to whatever we saw in the lake a few days ago, which meant I would be able to move the eggs and cause a distraction. That was the idea at least—to give me and Megan cover to run away." His face contorted into disparity. "But she never showed up. Only you did."

"I'm so, so sorry about Megan. I really am. But pissing off the lake monster isn't going to fix anything, and it's definitely not going to bring her back." Nothing I said changed his experience, so I gambled. "Besides, what about all that stuff you were telling me in the shed about those people who hurt you and the life you were going to build? You can still run away and I won't stop you! Go start fresh."

The gamble didn't pay off. "It's not the same without her, and all of those assholes will still be out there, free to fuck up the world as they please." A twisted smile found its way back to his place. "Expect for one. I told you on day one, Eddie, that this year was going to be war."

My feet demanded I start to inch backward, being mindful not to bump into an egg while keeping my face to him. "We're friends, right? Let's just talk. Friends can talk, and we'll figure something out. Yeah?"

"Friends?" Dexter took a full step toward me while he grimaced at the word. "You have been the biggest thorn in my side since the day we met. Year after year, I have to show up at this god-forsaken camp to see your face. Mr. Popular with his group of fuck-wads."

"I don't know what you mean."

"Don't play dumb, Eddie. You know exactly what I mean. Every year I try to make a few new friends, and you just have to show up and take me down a peg. You tell them that I'm dumb, embarrass me in front of the girls, or try to one-up me. Hell, even when I try to beat you to the punch, you get the best of me, and I'm sick of it."

I inched another half step backwards and felt my foot brush against something solid. "You think I'm your bully? You've tortured me day in and day out since we met."

"Because you deserved it. Hell, even with Anna Richards, you couldn't let me win. I tried to stop you and tell you it was a bad plan, but you didn't listen to me. You never listen, Eddie! It's always your way or the highway."

Was he right? I tried to pull up the memories, but they all felt scrambled, like they'd been chopped up and glued together out of order. If he really tried to stop my prank that almost killed Anna, why didn't he say so when we talked about it after our shift in the Mess Hall? Maybe he was trying to keep his cool guy persona going, or maybe he didn't care enough to correct me. Had I really caused him so much pain, just like he did to me, or was I just viewing it that way to justify my actions? Then a name popped into my head, proving his point: June.

The first time I met Dexter was at drop-off our first year. His mom parked her fade yellow sedan half on the curb in front of my mom's van. Our mother had gotten into a bickering contest each other's parking jobs. Dexter had tried to sneak away from the embarrassing display and his mother cried out 'Dexter June Hansley' and I couldn't help but snicker. I told everyone I met, because it was something to talk about, and that made me feel big. From that moment one we took turns going at each other.

Maybe he was right about me afterall. Maybe.

"I am so sorry, Dexter." I kneeled down and placed my hand on a palm-sized rock that my foot had felt. "But none of that makes this okay."

"I warned you, day one, it's fucking war." He pressed the words out through a locked jaw.

It looked like he was about to rush toward me, so in the middle of his half-step, I pulled my arm back and threw the rock as hard as I could. I hit him just above his left eye, which caused him to let out a scream and stumble back—back toward the slick, dark corner of the room. He lost his footing and stumbled toward the shape, until he hit into the it and a pair of bright green orbs sprung open behind his head.

They were bright enough to light up the whole space, and suddenly I could see what happened. Dexter had fallen onto the head of the lake monster, the same monster that I saw coming toward me in the water and the same one that I saw erupt onto the beach and devour Diego. It opened its mouth, revealing its needle-like teeth and letting out a wet growl. Dexter let out a scream of his own, but it was short-lived; the monster didn't hesitate to twist its neck around and chomp Dexter nearly in half. All I could do was watch as the creature lifted Dexter's flaring legs off the ground and slowly pulled his whole body into its throat.

My fight or flight mechanism kicked it, and I bolted for the exit, not daring to scream, speak, or even breathe as I did. I tucked through the smaller tunnel, sprinting across the main burrow, and scrambled on my hands and knees to climb up the entrance tunnel until I reached the surface. When I emerged, I was met with a spotlight on my face, but I didn't stop. I'd been above ground for less than a second when I heard that wet roar from behind me, so I bolted toward the light.

A voice called out from behind the light, "Eddie, don't stop running! Don't look back!" I didn't listen.

I looked back and saw the thing rushing up the tunnel behind me, with its two giant eyes fixed on me. I screamed out, "Help me!" I didn't know what to expect or even what anyone could do, but then I heard five shots ring out.

My legs didn't stop moving, and I didn't dare look back another time. I pushed across the small chuck of the island until I reached a boat and pulled myself onboard. Everything was blurry, and my vision was full of floaters, so I couldn't see a thing, but I felt someone grab me by the arm and yank me to one side.

"I've had enough of your shit, kid." A voice said.

"Ranger, stand down." Another voice demanded, followed by a thud and peircing pain in the back of my head. "I said stand down!" The voice demanded again, but it didn't matter. I slipped into the black pretty quickly after that.

You've Got A Deal

I must have been in a liminal space between sleep and daydream because I saw fragments so vivid during that spell that I could have mistaken them for memories. Voices faded in and out, sometimes sounding like old friends and other times sounding like strangers of the aggravated variety. There were sensations, some light, some intense, all over my body like I was being poked, prodded, and hauled. It was uncomfortable to say the least.

My mind drifted to the last few words Dexter had said to me, revealing that I was just as much a stain on his life as he was mine. I had no clue how broken and toxic his home life was, but in hindsight, I suppose I should have expected it; people aren't born evil. From what little life experience I had up to that point, I figured evil was forged, or maybe planted, into someone. Just like my mother, she didn't start off terrible, but I'd seen my grandmother's mean side enough to suppose that some of that hatred had rubbed off on her daughter and some more would rub off on me.

That made me wonder about Rodney and how suddenly he abandoned me, even choosing to lean into the theory that I was the one who killed Barry. When he first proposed the idea that I could have somehow murdered my friends, I thought he'd lost his marbles, or maybe he was so scared that he'd rather throw me under the bus than risk getting run over by it himself. But after hearing what Dexter had to say, it made me doubt. Had I been a bad friend? Bad enough to lead Rodney to think I was capable of robbing the world of Barry?

I replayed memory after memory from our summers together, and dreamed every 'what-if' that my dazed mind could conjure. Through the years I viewed myself as the victim, the helpless kid whose parents couldn't be bothered with him, so they shipped him off. Through my eyes I was the castaway, the kids too awkward to get the girl, an outsider amongst outsiders - the prodigal son determined to prove the masses wrong. But was any of it true? Did it matter?

Each of us, every kid that stepped on the shores of Lake Alkali, found ourselves there for a host of reasons. Some looked forward to it, others dreaded it; regardless, we ended up there. We put the ongoing story of our home lives on hold for a week to play pretend, to get a do-over, to be someone that maybe we weren't allowed to be at home. In that way, I suppose none of us actually knew each other; we only knew the versions we put on display. For all I knew, Rodney might go by a different name in Boston. I only knew the Rodney that he wanted me to see.

Eventually, after drifting in that liminal state for what must have been hours, my brain and body started to find each other again and my eyes began to flicker open. Someone was waiting for me.

"About fucking time."

"Huh?" I managed to groan out as my eyes wrestled their way back to function.

"You're in some deep shit Mr. Matthews, real deep shit." The voice hissed. "Honestly though I should thank you, if you would've ran off and gotten yourself killed, that would have been quite the setback for me."

Finally, I was able to keep my eyes open and draw in sight. My hands were above my head, and I could feel something tied between my wrists, like I'd been bound. I was sitting, though, against a wood-paneled wall. The air smelled stale, with tangles of wood smoke and rot mixed in, and then it hit me—it was the small cabin we'd found, where Barry was killed.

"Holy shit." The words broke out of me like a reflex and my whole body jolted as I tried to pull my arms free.

"Hey now, just calm down." The voice came from a man kneeling in front of the shack's wood stove. "I'd hate for you to end up like your friend." The stranger, with his back still to me, stretched his arm to the side and pointed at Barry.

His body was still there, skin sunken in, eyes removed, with flies buzzing around him. I wanted to puke, but only managed another, "Holy fucking shit!"

"I said simmer down." The stranger stood up, grabbed a book off one of the shelves, and chuckled it at me, hitting me square in the nose. Blood started to rush down my face, reminding me of the warm, wet feeling of Barry's own blood between my fingers when I failed to save him. "Look what you made me do."

My vision was spotty from the impact of the book, but as the stranger turned around, I saw a shape that surprised me. The wide brim of a hat. "Ranger?" I asked, my voice shaky from the panic in my chest.

They stepped closer, and kneeled down next to me. It was Murph. "Surprise."

"Murph?" My voice cracked as I asked.

"In the flesh." He stood up, went to a stool across from me and sat down. "You have no idea how thankful I am that you woke up. I hit you harder than I expected too, and got a bit worried."

"I don't understand. What's happening?" I began sucking in breaths of air, feeling like my lungs were going to pop.

Murph raised his hands up, and motioned for me to calm down. "Nothing serious, I just have some questions for you Eddie."

"Lawyer." I blurted out, thinking of how brave Rodney had seemed when he demanded the same thing back in the office cabin. "I need a lawyer."

Murph shook his head, drew his gun from his holster and slung in gingerly from one finger. "No dice Eddie. This is a, shall we call it unofficial, interview. Understand?"

"Listen Murph, I don't know what you want, but I swear I don't got it." I swallowed a bit of blood while I spoke, the taste of rust washed over my tongue causing me to wince.

"That's not what Rodney said." He gripped the gun and pointed it toward me. "Rodney says you've got exactly what I'm after."

I swallowed hard and tried to calm my nerves. "What? What do I have?"

Murph cracked a smile, and his eyes gleamed behind his wire glasses. "I want what's mine, Mr. Matthews. No more, no less."

"I don't understand." I said, finally building the courage to match his gaze.

His smile collapsed into a scowl. "I ain't in the mood for playing dumb." He got up, stepped over me, and pulled me up by a rope he'd tied around my wrists. "I got to show you something."

I wanted to fight, even though I knew it wasn't good sense too, but my spirit was broken and my body was worn out. Murph led me by the rope out the shack's tiny front door into the woods. It was daylight out, and the sun seemed to be headed west, meaning it had to be sometime in the afternoon - which also meant I'd been passed out for nearly half a day or more. That thought scared me.

I'd only seen that patch of woods in the dark and was struck by how dense it was. A mixture of elm, tall pine, post oak and ash trees clustered together like islands in a sea of foliage, with each variety keeping to its kind. The air was thick with humidity and the light was tinted green from the canopy of leaves that nearly blocked out the sky. I'd seen nothing like it in the rest of the forests around camp.

Murph yanked the rope to get me to stop gawking and led me around the shack. We walked into the woods for a good thirty feet when a lone tree stood out to me, separating itself from the others. A wide willow tree had a long branch that jutted out to one side, and from that branch hung a person.

"Fucking hell." I muttered as Murph drug me closer to the tree.

He didn't acknowledge me, he just kept walking. As we approached the details came into view. Cargo shorts, high socks and hiking boots adorned the body's legs. A brown shirt, stained with blots of deep red was buttoned over their torso - It was Sabrina. Her face blue from suffocation and her hands duct taped behind her back.

"See?" Murph nodded at her corpse. "That Barry kid got off easy compared to my partner here. These are the kinds of things that can happen when I don't get what I want."

I started to hyperventilate again. "I don't, uh, don't understand," was all I could will myself to say.

He turned around and whipped me with the butt of his pistol, causing my knees to give out, sending me to the ground. "How do you not understand? Answer my questions or die! It's simple! Got it?"

My ears began to ring, and I wondered if it was from the blow to the head or if the monster was causing it somehow, like Barry had suggested. Either way, it didn't matter; I was stunned, and gathering my thoughts was exhausting. "I don't understand why you are doing this. Just tell me what you want."

Murph knelt down to my level and placed the barrel of his gun against my shoulder. "Tell me where you hid my fucking money."

It hit me all at once. The money, the cocaine, the grave, Barry being shot, Lester being stabbed, Levi being beat to death, and Olivia's drowning—it was all connected. My friends and I had kicked a hornet's nest and hadn't even known it.

I started to laugh, I couldn't help it, it was a reflex. "You think murdering folks is worth six grand?" I asked between snickers. "You're fucking crazy."

His eyes narrowed behind his glasses, and he pressed the gun harder against me. "It's not about the money, kid. Rodney told us that you buried it, and only you know where, so where is it?"

"I can't tell you." I said, still coming down from my laughing fit.

"Why not?" He growled.

There's a story about people who see their lives flash before their eyes during near-death experiences, but I didn't have that experience with Murph or even the monster, for that matter. Instead, I felt calm, and I saw pathways, like I was being given one final choice to make before my number was up. The options I saw weren't complex, but they were clear, and my gut told me I wouldn't get a do-over if I chose wrong.

"Because if I do, you'll just kill me." I looked up at him and felt an insane, unhinged, unwarranted smile appear on my face. "That's why we're out here, right? In the middle of nowhere." His eyes widened, and he stood up, looking down and bewildered. "You killed the other too, didn't you? Why?"

He took his gun and adjusted the bill of his Ranger's cap with it. "They got in the way."

"So you're part of those robberies that happened? You're S.M., aren't you? What's the S stand for?"

"Seth." He grunted. "How'd you figure that out?"

"I found a note on the island for you from L.D. and G.F. It seems you were helping them move cocaine, and a lot of it." I spat out a mouthful of blood. "You know, it looks like you have something I want."

He furrowed his brow and put his hands on his hips—his superman stance, as I'd seen him do before. "Yeah? What's that?"

"Answers. " I managed my way to my feet and rubbed some of the blood on my face with my bound hands. "How about a trade? You answer my questions, and I'll bring you to the cashbox."

He thought for a second, rolling his eyes back and forth like he was arguing with someone in his head, before he raised his gun and pointed it at me again. "How about I just kill you now and save myself a headache?"

"You could," Some madman took over my body momentarily and willed my body to press my forehead against his gun. "but I'm willing to bet you won't."

"Why's that?" He pressed the barrel on my forehead and twisted it.

"You said it yourself; losing me would have been a setback for you. My guess is that you're going to peg Barry's, Diego's, and Megan's deaths on me. Maybe we even add on Levi's and Olivia's for good messure. Rodney handed you an easy scapegoat when he said he didn't see what I saw, which gave you the cover you needed. I don't know how you plan on explaining Lester and Sabrina." His eyes widened at their names. "But I imagine you've already got your hands full with that." I pushed my forehead against the gun again. "So are you going to kill me, or do we have a deal?"

I felt the barrel of the gun shake against my skin before Murph pulled it away and let out a grunt. "Fine. You got a deal."

Poetry In Motion

A series of compromises were discussed and debated between the two of us; some were long shots, others made sense, but ultimately I improved my situation just enough to give me some sense of hope. The rope that was used to tie my hands was removed, and the burns underneath were cleaned with rubbing alcohol from a first aid kit that had a half inch of dust on top before being bound again, but with standard handcuffs instead. I talked my way into a meal of canned beans and bottled water, the first thing I'd eaten in what seemed like days, which was followed up by cleaning and bandaging the fresh cut on my head.

I was only able to talk Murph into that list of demands because I was truly in such poor shape. But it also gave me an opportunity to pine for more information than I think he'd wanted to share. Growing up, I learned that my mother couldn't stop talking while she was doing something with her hands. If you wanted to learn who was cheating on who or what she really thought of Becker's new summer house, all you had to do was ask her while she was making dinner.

As Murph went to work patching me up and feeding me, I asked him about the murders, the motives, and the history of the whole scheme. It turned out that Murph, like most of us, didn't come from the most stable home life. He was originally from Hay Springs, a near-ghost town not far off from the

Nebraska National Forest, and when he was a kid, he always dreamed of being a big city cop. So as soon as he got the chance, he jumped out to Denver, joined the force, and got hit with a shitstick after a shitstick. Never chosen for promotion, always getting traffic duty, and rarely seeing any kind of action.

One day though he gets a call, his mother is sick, and she was such a bitch to her children during their lives that none of them will put up with her, except Murph. He was the youngest and felt a kinship with her that his siblings didn't, so he accepted his fate and moved home. The problem was that there was no need for a cop in Hay Springs, but he did see an opening for a Park Ranger, so he took it. Murph was dealt a bad hand, and he was trying to make the best of it until he got a call.

He made a friend in Denver, a guy he only referred to as Chuck, who found a lucrative side gig setting up safe passage for drug traffickers through and around Colorado. Chuck said there were some new players in the game that wanted a route far off the beaten path, and western Nebraska is the closest thing you can find to no man's land, so he wanted to know if Murph was open to it. Between the mounting medical bills for his mother and the debt he found himself in from his failed stint in Denver, Murph felt like he couldn't turn it down.

Chuck told him to pick a set of highways and to find a safe house in case things ever went sideways, so Murph did just that and found an old hunting shack, the one we were in, that had been left to rot for some time. He spent his nights and weekends hiking out to do repairs until it was functioning again. Once he was happy with that, he started poking around at the Ranger's station to figure out the 'dead zones' until he mapped what he thought was the perfect route for someone to use who wanted to not be seen.

Everything went fine for about a year, and then one day Murph hears from one of his clients, a man called Three-Bone, who said that the DEA was onto him, he'd been spotted, and he needed to drop the product without delayed arrival in Denver. Murph came up with a plan; he had two regulars who used his routes, the mysterious L.D. and G.F., who were always looking for another score. So he approached them with an offer.

Take the drugs, but hit a series of gas stations along the route to make authorities think it's a robbery spree. Three-Bone would drop the product at the first planned robbery, L.D and G.F would pick it up and then start their string of stick-ups. The idea was to keep the heat on Three-Bone but remove the product. Hopefully the DEA would waste their time tracking Three-Bone, who would, technically, be clean, while the Nebraska State Patrol debated if a string of no-mans-land robberies was worth their time. Unfortunately for them, it was a bad plan.

The DEA caught onto the swap, and the State Patrol was quick to respond. Murph's associates, L.D. and G.F., demanded to use the safe house, but Murph was worried it'd blow the whole operation. He told them to head into the forrest and look for somewhere to hide; apparently, he'd come across a handful of old buildings and crumbling homesteads while working for the Rangers, and he had faith they'd find one. One problem arose, though; he never figured out where. Neither did the DEA or State Patrol, but when Chuck told him that

L.D. and G.F. never arrived in Denver, Murph knew the worst had happened.

"So you just quit looking?" I asked, struggling to eat beans out of a can with a spoon while handcuffed.

"No, it was just hard to find the time. I still had to show up and do my job during the day, and being out here at night came with its own challenges."

"But that changed when Lester called you guys?"

He nodded while pulling at his mustache. "That was like kicking a hornets nest."

After Murph rode out to the island with Downs and saw the shed on the island, he knew that must be the place his associate had hidden. The problem, of course, was the 'animal disturbance' we encountered and the psychotic break that Downs apparently had in his office after encountering the thing. Murph knew he'd Downs to find the island again, so after he cuffed him and removed him from camp, he told him that they'd take a canoe and go look for the monster again, just the two of them. Downs was all for it; he was worked up from his past run-in with the thing and was looking for some sort of payback. He realized though that Downs' zeal would be a problem, so once they'd navigated to the island, Murph drove a knife into his chest.

"This knife?" I asked as I fumbled it from my belt loop.

Murph looked at it in awe. "Well, fuck, yeah, that's it. You really found him?"

I nodded, trying to keep the image of his sun-bloated body from my mind. "What about the others?"

"You really want me to keep going? To keep telling you about the people I killed?"

A chill ran up my spine. He said it so calmly, and as a matter of fact, I hated it. "I need answers."

"Suit yourself." He sighed and put the knife back in belt loop. "A memento for you."

He said he left Downs strapped into the canoe on the beach before going straight for the shack. Inside, he found nothing, but he didn't get to look around as much as he wanted before he heard a scream. Outside, Levi and Olivia had made landfall in their own canoe; they were out looking for Diego and Megan and had decided to check the island. They'd found Down's body and were on high alert. When Murph approached them, Levi pulled out a knife and demanded an explanation. He didn't go into details, but the two of them got into a scuffle that ended with Levi being struck in the back of the head with a rock.

Olivia tried to help but didn't do much, so she decided to make a run for it by hijacking the canoe that Murph had taken up. He rushed after her into the tides and drug her out of the boat and into the water by her hair. Murph swears he didn't mean to drown her, but that it 'just sort of happened' and in the process he lost the boat that Downs was strapped down in. Luckily for Murph, though, the canoe Levi and Olivia had used was still beached.

He hauled Levi into the boat and back up to the shack, which he said was a task and a half given the storm that was starting to break out. The plan was to question him. Murph didn't know he was the camp maintenance man; he figured he'd learn more through some interrogation. Murph hadn't gotten a chance to do anything when he wasn't interrupted by screaming (I figure it was when Megan went over the ledge—her last moment), so he went to go investigate.

While he was out looking for the source of the scream, the rain began to pour down—the same rain Barry, Rodney, and I found ourselves in. When he couldn't find the source of the scream he hoofed it back to his shack, but when we arrived, he saw the door open and a shadow outside. Murph said he just sat in the trees and watched for a while, wondering what was going on and questioning how someone found his safe house. Then I poked my head out to call Barry in. Once Murph saw there was more than one of us, he feared that all of us, Levi and Olivia included, were a part of some undercover group looking for his product, so he pulled the trigger.

As for why he didn't bury a bullet in Rodney and I, he didn't say; he only mentioned that the storm had gotten so bad that it was impossible to follow us. Murph said he was sure he was cooked and that once we were out of his reach, someone would come looking for him. But then he heard word at the station that two kids showed up with a beaten body at Camp Alkali, and he saw one last chance to wrap his head around what was happening.

"Then Rodney handed me over to you on a silver platter, didn't he?"

Murph clicked his tongue. "I couldn't have planned it better myself. I was sweating like a pig while you boys drove Sabrina up a tree, and then along comes Rodney, volunteering to be a star witness in naming little Eddie Matthews a murderer. Poetry in motion, I tell you what."

"And what about Sabrina? She got wise to you?"

"Not really. She was so obsessed with solving the mystery of my missing associates that she never knew I was under her nose. Well, until that whole thing on the boat." He adjusted his hat and looked off to one side, reliving the memory. "I just couldn't believe you were alive, and I knew I couldn't let you slip again. I pistol whipped you, she lost her shit, and those two kids just kept squealing."

My gut twisted at that, and a small fire lit in my mind. "What kids?"

His twisted smile crept back onto his face. "Right. I almost forgot about them." He jumped to his feet and pushed out the door. "Hop to it, Mr. Matthews, your friends are waiting."

I scrambled to my feet and chased after him into the green light of the forest. "What friends?" The small fire flickered and flashed into an inferno. "Answer me!"

Murph turned around, his gun drawn again, and pointed to my stomach. "To be honest, Eddie, I think you've gotten enough answers so it's time to hold up your end of the deal. But, because I'm feeling generous, I'll give you one more. Our mutual friend Rodney is the first, and then there was the other one, the girl." He tapped his foot and mumbled, "What was her name? Kimi? Kathy?" Murph snapped his finger and pointed to the sky. "Kaya, that's right. She was worried sick about you."

Big Fish Eat Little Fish

Murph marched me through the forrest down to the covered dock that Levi had shown us boys in The Hole, monologuing as he went about how turning in all that missing product would get him back in Chuck's good graces. He was itching to start making good money again, and he didn't bother keeping that fact to himself. Desperation and low moral fiber make for a dangerous mix, even among the meekest of us.

Once the dock was in sight, I saw Rodney and Kaya, with their hands tied up like mine had been, tied to a work table. Neither of them looked like they'd been beaten or pistol-whipped, but I could see the exhaustion and fear on their faces. They were sleeping as we approached, and even in sleep, I could see their clenched jaws and sunken eyes. I wanted to run to them to check on them, but the entire time we were walking, Murph was sure to keep the nose of his pistol pressed against my back. I wasn't good to anyone dead.

"Rise and shine, munchkins." Murph said in a sing-song voice before tapping Rodney's head with his gun. "I brought ya'll a playmate."

Both of them took a moment to wake up and take charge of their eyes, but once they did, they shared the same shocked expression.

"Oh my god." Rodney gasps.

"What happened to you, Eddie?" Kaya asked, pulling herself to her feet and pulling against her bindings, trying to get to me. "Are you okay? Did he do this?" She shot Murph a death glare so cold that it would've made God himself shiver.

"Simmer down, little miss." Murph said, grabbing my shoulder and pulling me back from her. "He's breathing, ain't he? How about you just count your lucky stars while you still have some?"

He loaded each of us at gunpoint onto a boat that I didn't recognize. It was an inflatable raft with a decent-sized engine, a spotlight rack, and the Nebraska Game and Parks logo painted on one side. Stepping on board didn't give me hope that it'd hold water, but I didn't figure Murph would be receptive to my criticizing of his vessel.

Murph seemed to lose his chatty nature once we were out on the water, which was a welcomed change. I was getting tired of his voice. The blue sky and clear sun that had illuminated the forest's green air was darkening, and the light breeze that had cut through the humidity had started picking up speed, but most damning of all, the well-known omen of buzzing in my ears was back. Kaya was twisting her face in discomfort, and Rodney was rocking his head side to side—it wasn't just in my head.

We'd been sitting in the back of the boat, next to the engine, while Murph piloted it from a wheel at the ship's nose, so I dared to speak, hoping he couldn't hear me. I leaned closer to Rodney and asked, "You hear it too, don't you?"

He nodded.

"What is it?" Kaya asked through gritted teeth. "It hurts."

"It's the lake monster." Rodney said, his eyes fixed on the water as we sliced through it.

"You're joking." Kaya waited for a response that didn't come. "Aren't you?"

"I told you it was real. It's not my fault you didn't believe me." I quipped. "We need a plan."

"I know." Rodney agreed. "You think we can overpower him?"

Kaya gasped loud enough that I thought Murph was going to hear her, but he didn't turn around. "Just give him what he wants, and then it'll all be over."

Rodney broke his stare at the water and peered at Kaya. "You can't be that stupid."

"He's just going to kill us after he's got what he needs." I said as a clap of thunder rang out, and a streak of lightning lit up the sky above us. "If we even make it that far."

Kaya was looking at the water ahead of us when her jaw began to shudder. "Guys, what is that?"

Two giant green orbs were heading toward the boat, and I had an idea. "You guys trust me?"

Kaya looked back at me, her jaw still shaking. "Why?"

"Because if you don't, this is going to seem really stupid." I wiggled the knife in my belt loop free and handed it to Rodney. "Get yourselves loose, and get her somewhere safe. Understand?"

Rodney took the knife and nodded with weariness eyes. I managed to get to my feet and looked over the boat's interior for something to use, but found nothing. My mind slowed the world around me, and I had another one of those moments where I could see only two options, and both of them looked like points of no return. That was okay with me.

I leaped across the short distance from where I stood to where Murph was piloting the boat and got my cuffs over his head and around his neck. "Stand down! Or we go overboard."

He reached back with his hands, trying to claw at me, but didn't have to reach. Murph was sputtering and gasping but managed to say, "Fuck you."

I noticed his right hand go for his holster, and Rodney rushed over just in time for him to snatch it away. He walked back toward Kaya, who was untied but still sitting by the engine, covering her ears. The ringing had grown to a near roar, but one that I'd become accustomed to, and rain had begun to come down.

"Fuck you, kids!" Murph yelled as he began to overpower me. "I'm not going out like this." He began to kick against my legs, trying to drive me to the edge of the boat.

A loud, wet growl rose up from the water behind me, and I craned my neck to see those green eyes looking up at me, seeming to beckon to me. Kaya saw them and cried out, "Eddie, be careful!"

Looking into those eyes bobbing under the water, I felt something call out to me. I felt it when I encountered them under the water too, after going overboard with Lester and Murph for the first time. The eyes didn't show me empathy or compassion, but they did seem intelligent. I knew they were intelligent enough to know that I was not a threat and that I was not there to bother it. Still, they were also the eyes that killed my friends; they couldn't be ignored, but in that moment, I either let Murph loose and risked him taking hold of the situation again or I chose the nuclear option.

I pulled as tightly as I could and crossed my hands, choking Murph as hard as I could. "Rodney," I barked, "you tell them I didn't do it, okay? Promise me you'll tell them the truth."

"Eddie, don't be crazy." He said, taking a step toward me.

Another growl rose up, causing the boat's rubber bottom to rumble. "Promise me!"

"Okay, okay, I promise." His voice shook.

"Eddie," Kaya was standing by then, about a step and a half from where I was, "don't do it."

My eyes darted between her and Rodney before settling on Rodney. "Get her a life jacket, alright? She can't swim." I looked back at Kaya and gave her a wink; it was the only movie star thing I could think to do. Even in the face of death, I had to impress the girl.

"You're going to regret..." Murph began to say this before I pulled us overboard into the storming waters of Lake Alkali and watched the boat speed away from us as we sank.

We drifted downward for long enough to the water to grow dark. I thought I could hold onto him once we hit the water, but it became clear that the monster was more interested in him than I was, because by the glow of its luminous eyes approaching, I watched as its tail wrapped around his torso and began to pull. Murph had lost his hat and glasses when we went overboard, and I could see his wild eyes panicking in the green glow. He punched the monster in its snout, kicked it in its snob horn, and clawed at the tail that had locked onto him.

I watched for what felt like hours, but it could have only been seconds, while Murph struggled to escape his fate. While

I watched, I realized that this thing, this monster, wasn't all that different from any other animal. It rushed at me for being near its burrow; it attacked Dexter for invading its home and threatening its eggs; it took Diego and Megan for prey because to a creature as large as it humans are probably prey. Animals are capable of neither cruelty nor selfishness, only surival.

Murph was the real monster. He laid in wait for others to lead him to what he'd lost, and he was willing to trade human life for progress toward his goal. Men, women, and children were all fair game to him, even though he was supposedly evolved enough to care about the difference. And there he was, falling victim to a natural cycle he likely never considered or thought of. Big fish eat little fish, and big monsters eat little ones. Poetry in motion, as Murph would've said.

The monster had its jaws latched into Murph's leg, spirals of blood flowed from the wounds, when a sound ripped through the water. A wet growl, higher pitched than the ones I'd heard, and farther off. Whatever made that sound must have beckoned to the monster, because it whipped its head in the direction of the noise so fast that it ripped one of Murph's legs from his body and swam off in a hurry.

I did my best to swim upwards once it was gone, which was hard with my hands still cuffed, but I managed to find the surface. My lungs gasped for air as soon as they were able, and to my suprise Rodney pulled me into the boat in a hurry. Both he and Kaya wrapped me up in a thermal blanket they'd found in the first aid kit while clamoring for me with questions I couldn't make out. They may have gone on forever like that; if a hand hadn't tried to pull itself into the boat, it was Murph.

I looked over the edge and could see the trail of blood in the water from where his leg had been attached. "You got to help me, kid. Please." His voice was weak, and his face was flushed.

"Do I?"

"Come on, Eddie." He coughed and sputtered. "You're a better person than I am. Don't let this chance pass to prove it."

"Am I?" I looked at Rodney. "You still got that knife?"

"Oh, uh, yeah." He fished it from his pocket. "Here."

I flicked the blade open and squeezed it in my right fist so hard that my knuckles went white. "Seth, right? That's your first name."

He groaned. "Yes, yes. My name is Seth."

"Good. Well, Seth, I don't think you know me as well as you think." I rose my fist and drove it down into his back, digging the knife into the meat of his shoulder. "Here's a memento for you." Murph let go of the boat's side and sank into the water.

I watched as he drifted downward and wondered, no I hoped to be honest, that the monster would come back for him. Big monsters eat little monsters. It just seemed right.

None of us spoke while Rodney piloted the boat back to camp. The weather began to clear once the monster swam off to answer whatever call it had heard, so navigating our way back was easier than we expected. When we arrived, we were greeted with a dozen vehicles with flashing red and blue lights, paramedics, cops, and, of course, Park Rangers.

It turned out that Levi didn't survive his injuries, so between that and finding Olivia's drowned body, the county sheriff ordered everyone he could spare to lock down Camp

Alkali and the National Forest. When we pulled up, they had dozens of questions, some of which we could answer and others we couldn't. None of the answers really mattered, though, because once word got out that a lake monster had killed three campers, headlines took a strange turn.

The half-dead folk tale about the Lake Alkali Monster had new life breathed into it. For years after, people would claim to have seen it, and a whole new generation of campfire stories were born from it. The monster even got a new, more scientific-sounding name, Giganticus Brutervious, which never really caught on. People rarely talk about the murders, drug trafficking, or the terrible things that happened to a group of kids that they'd never really come back from. Stories like that don't make for good headlines.

As for myself, I didn't share anything that day; I was still processing. I was ushered to an ambulance that waited near the beach, where a nice lady took my vitals and looked over my new collections of bruises, scars, and stitches. While I was being checked out, a grizzled man in a State Patrolmen's uniform came over to me with a small notebook in hand.

"Are you doing okay, son?" He huffed.

I actually thought about his question for a moment, because I doubted that I was, but I also knew he probably didn't care. He was there for answers; I understood that. "Been better, been worse."

"You don't say?" He raised an eyebrow. "I talked to your friends over there." He pointed to Rodney and Kaya, who were sitting on the hood of a patrol car a ways off, "and they said you might have some things you'd like to share."

"You don't say?" I chuckled at myself; he seemed less amused.

"Right, well, what can you tell me about Ranger Murphy?" He asked, pulling his notepad to his face.

"Lawyer." I said, flashing a look over at Rodney. He flashed one back.

"Excuse me?" He pulled the notebook away and leveled a glare at me.

"Lawyer."

Milton Keynes UK
Ingram Content Group UK Ltd.
UKHW042055240924
448733UK00006B/306

9 798227 283283